LANCELOT
KING BAN'S SON OF BENOIC

HARVEY W. BERGER

ISBN 1-456-46601-1

Printed in the United States of America

For Me

So that at least one of my stories
will be seen in print

and

with great expectations,

For my Grandchildren,
Isaac, Josiah, Eliot, Hosea and Rebecca

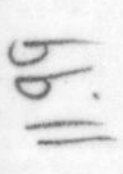

ACKNOWLEDGEMENT
OF THE DEAD

Nennius, 8th century, "History of the Britons,"
Translated by J.A. Giles

Geoffrey of Monmouth, 12th century, "History of the
Kings of Britain," Translated by Lewis Thorpe

Author unknown, 13th century, "The Death of Arthur,"
Translated by James Cable

Author unknown, "Lancelot of the Lake (Prose Cycle),"
13th century, Translated by Corin Corley

Sir Thomas Malory, 15th century, "Le Morte d'Arthur,"

SPECIAL THANKS TO THE LIVING

My wife, Sally Ann
My daughter, Marni Lynn

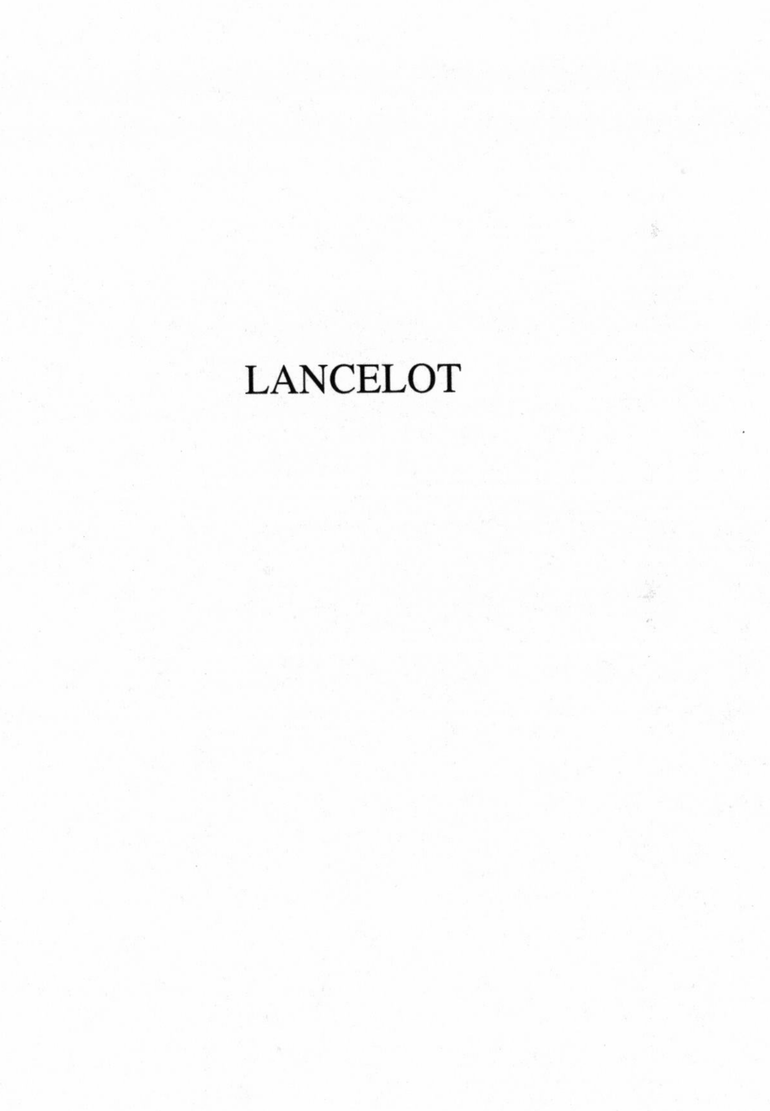

LANCELOT

Chapter 1

My palfrey picked her way slowly down the hill with hardly any guidance from me while my escort of eight heavily armed lancers followed at a distance. They were now at ease since we were out of the forest and so close to Holy Isle that there was no longer any danger of highwaymen or rogue knights. Contrariwise, the closer we came to our objective the more nervous and apprehensive I became. It was four days since we left Carlisle and soon I would have no choice but to carry out my assigned task. Waiting for me was Sir Lancelot of the Lake, the greatest knight in all of Christendom, infamous for his hot temper, furious rage and headless bodies strewn about. Still, I took some small comfort in remembering that he was an old man now and if I angered him or offended him in any way I could escape him and it would probably not be at the cost of my life.

My name is Lonmarch. Our blessed Queen Vivyan, the recent bride of King Constantine, charged me to put the story of the great man's life on parchment. The gossip is that she befriended him when she was a very young maiden, that he had been very gallant to her and done her some great service and that she had fallen in love with him. Now she wanted the truth of his life written down before others could tarnish his memory with innuendos and lies. The Queen has sent me, her secretary, because I am a scribe and because I have an uncanny memory that retains everything I hear with complete faithfulness. She also thinks that I am intelligent, sensible, thoughtful and trustworthy, all of which, in my sincere humility, I aver that I am. Nevertheless, this responsibility is a great trust and honor placed in me, and the likelihood of failure fills me with much concern.

By mid-day we arrived at the town of Fenwick where my escort was to find lodging and wait for me as long as necessary. Then I found a local, with a small boat, who rowed me, at low tide, to Holy Isle. For the few coins I gave him, he carried my pack filled with parchments, ink and pens, and led me to the gates of the priory. I promised him further payment if he came back every day at low tide until I was ready to return to Fenwick. He agreed and when he was gone I rang a bell and was soon greeted by a monk who silently led me to the Abbot who was well aware of my mission.

To say that I was shocked the first time I saw Sir Lancelot would be a great understatement. He was not a shriveled, bent, old man. He stood straight as a lance and though he appeared to be thin, energy and strength seemed to accompany his every move. His eyes were clear and his glance intense but at the same time curious and a bit merry. His hair was thin, as one might expect, but it still had much of the bright gold color that so many women had talked about. His voice was strong and he made me welcome immediately. His offer of an almost bone-crushing handshake made me feel like a compatriot rather a servant before his master. After escorting me around the monastery he took me to a comfortable room which would be my lodging and where he would tell me his story while I wrote and listened.

The next morning, after Matins, he came to my room and we began.

"My lord," I said, "there are old stories about how you came by your name. What is the truth of it?"

"Ah, Lonmarch, that is a question easily answered. But if I tell you outright there is little to be gained from the answer itself. Let us strike a bargain. I shall tell you what I know of my life, in my own way, and you shall write down what you will."

"My lord, that is a generous bargain which I humbly accept."

"Well, then, let us begin."

I am known as Lancelot but that was not my given name. The Lady Niniane who raised me from infancy, as a foster mother, called me Lancelot, which means "servant". She was known as the Lady of the Lake, because she is said to have mysteriously appeared in a boat on a lake and bestowed the sword Excalibur and its magical sheath on King Arthur. Many still believe that Niniane is my birth mother and that I was born and raised on an invisible island in the lake where Arthur received the sword. All of that is nonsense and superstition.

I did not know my true name and who my father and mother were until I was eighteen years old. I was more than twenty years old before I came to fully understand how my life had been planned and how I was manipulated to achieve a quest I knew nothing about.

What I do know about what happened before I was born, and before I was old enough to reliably remember, I learned from Merlin. More than anyone else except Niniane and her favorite, Saraide, Merlin knew more about me than anyone else living. My lodgings in Arthur's palace were close to Merlin's and we saw each other frequently. On many occasions, when the winter winds blew cold and the skies were a dark grey, we sought each other's companionship. When he was inclined to talk, I was an eager listener.

Now, Lonmarch, if you wish to understand my life, as I do, you must bear with me while I tell you a bit of history, some of which you may already know. I hope not to bore you too much before I tell about the glorious battles I have fought and the ladies I have known, about which you no doubt prefer to hear.

The Celts of Britain's ancient days were powerful and fearsome warriors. Although they constantly fought amongst themselves, no foreign nation ever succeeded in invading and settling their countries. That was true until the Emperors of the great Roman Empire cast their greedy eyes upon the jewel of the North Sea and finally conquered southern Britain.

For five hundred years the Romans occupied Britain and fought off invasions by Irish, Scots and Jutes, just as the Celts had done before them. During this long time of Roman dominion, the Britons became weak and cowardly. They were no longer a nation of warriors. When the Roman armies left Britain, foreign armies again invaded the country. Now the Britons were unable to defend themselves and pleaded for help from their ancestral cousins in Brittany. The Breton King sent his brother Constantine, who is no ancestor of your master, along with an army to drive the barbarians out of Britain.

Constantine succeeded and was made King of Britain but, after he died, the barbarian invasions were renewed. A British King named Vortigern encouraged Saxon mercenaries from Germany to come to Britain and make war on the barbarians in exchange for land and wealth. When the Saxons grew too numerous and powerful and threatened to overwhelm them, the

Britons turned to Constantine's sons, Ambrosius Aurelius and Uther, for help in expelling the Saxons.

For more than one hundred years after the Romans departed, Britain faced the ravages and destruction of almost constant war. Ambrosius and Uther were brave and victorious in battle but peace remained an elusive dream.

Niniane, was a High Priestess of the Druids. Her mother had told her the story of Bran, the son of Llyr, a giant who fought against the Irish long before there was a Britain. The Irish had a cauldron, which could cure the sick and wounded and raise the dead. Bran won the cauldron in battle and had his head placed on it because he was dying. He told his followers to bury his head in Londinium facing Gaul so that no invasion of our land would ever succeed. The ancient Britons believed that the Romans were able to conquer Britain only because the cauldron and Bran's head had been lost. According to the story, the holy relics could be found only by a knight of unequaled purity and prowess.

Niniane also heard the Irish priests talk about a man called Jesus who performed great miracles in a land called Judea. The Romans killed him, but he came back to life, and ascended to the heavens. Such powerful magic was seen, by many of his followers, as proof of his godhood.

One of Jesus' disciples was a man named Joseph of Arimathea. As blood dripped from a spear thrust in Jesus' side, Joseph collected some of it in silver cup which some now call the "Grail". It is still believed that because of the dried holy blood in the cup, it holds the god's magic and power. It is also supposed to be able to cure the sick and those wounded in battle and to raise the dead. The Irish priests say that whatever country possesses the cup and the holy blood dried within it, and gives it up to Jesus in heaven, can never be vanquished by a foreign foe.

The search for the cup has lasted more than five hundred years and still there is no knowledge of its hiding place. Followers of the new religion claim that when Joseph of Arimathea came to Britain from Gaul he built a castle that no ordinary man can find. They say that Joseph hid the cup in the castle and set many powerful knights to protect it. They defend the cup from evil men who would use it for their own purposes and from sinful men who cannot enter heaven and come before the face of god.

Like those who believed in Bran and the cauldron, those who believe in the Grail must find the bravest, strongest knight, who is completely pure of mind, spirit and body. Only he can find the castle. Only he has the physical strength and prowess to overcome the guardian knights. Then, that knight, who is without fear and beyond reproach, can ascend to heaven and return the cup with its holy blood to Jesus. Only when that is done, will Britain be safe, forever.

Many Druids, including Niniane, had stopped believing in the miracle of Bran and the cauldron. Yet her belief in magic, talismans and relics was unabated and she was sure of the power of the Grail even though she was not a follower of the new religion. After all, since so many had searched for the cup for so long, and still believed, how could it not be true? She saw her responsibility clearly. She was convinced that she was the one chosen to bring lasting peace to Britain and her people. She had to find the great pure knight and set him on the right path to completing the quest of the Grail.

My foster mother was not alone in her scheming. My dear friend Merlin was her willing tool in controlling the fate of the world. Although I cannot imagine him taking any of the Grail story seriously I can imagine him helping Niniane so that he would be privy to her schemes and also, perhaps for his own amusement or advantage.

In any case, when Uther Pendragon became King, Niniane and Merlin plotted for him to make a son who would be the great champion to find the Grail. But, Arthur was conceived in sin and his life was sinful. Oh, yes, he was brave and strong, and a great leader of kings and men, but he was weak and venal in so many ways.

By the time Arthur was crowned High King of Britain it had became obvious to Niniane that her hopes and plans for Arthur had been wasted and that her savior had to come from elsewhere.

Then her prayers to the gods for the perfect knight were answered.

Arthur, and the Kings who supported his claim to Uther's crown, faced and fought two enemies who threatened to overwhelm them; the Saxons who sought to subjugate and settle more land, and the other Kings of Britain who put their own squabbles aside and united in their opposition to Uther's "illegitimate" son. At Merlin's urging, Arthur sent to Brittany for assistance.

Two Kings came with their armies to Arthur's rescue. One was King Ban of Benoic and the other was his brother King Bohort of Ganis.

Merlin laughed when he told me about the first time Niniane saw King Ban. He said that she became so weak in the knees that she had to hold on to his arm for fear of falling. He felt her whole body shake and she gasped so for breath that she was close to swooning. But then, how could anyone blame her.

I give you my word, Lonmarch, that I do not boast about my sire. What I tell you now of King Ban is what Merlin related to me and what I repeat as truly as I am able. Suffice it to say that Merlin had a strange, far away and almost wistful look in his eyes when he talked about my Lord and how magnificent he was.

"Your father," Merlin said, "was taller and broader than most men and when he was astride his enormous white destrier he sat in the saddle as straight as a lance. His imposing presence was such that it was impossible for him to be unrecognized even in a field crowded with mounted knights. Wherever he moved, great numbers of knights moved with him. They were drawn to him, like moths to the flame, as if by his power or some other mysterious force. Eyes followed him everywhere hoping for a glance of recognition in return.

"He had thick flowing yellow hair that curled around the broadest shoulders I have ever seen. Powerful muscles stretched the clothing that covered him yet he moved as swiftly and as smoothly as an animal. His eyes were as blue as deep water and his smile, or grimace, were enough to elicit great joy or great terror, as he desired. He was the most beautiful and well-made man I had ever seen.

"But all of his demeanor and beauty was as nothing to his prowess in battle. Dressed in his armor he looked as if he were the god of war come to life. I saw him time and again ride into masses of knights and troops and cut them down as if he was cutting wheat with a scythe. The sight of him riding into battle drew cheers from Arthur's men and raised their spirits to the point of their being invincible. At the same time, I could hear a collective moan of despair from the enemy as they recognized that death and defeat were near at hand.

"The moment Niniane saw Ban of Benoic I surmised what her next scheme would be. She would at one stroke satisfy her lust for Ban and become the birth mother of the perfect knight. The Grail Knight, the savior of Britain, would have the courage and prowess of his father and the purity of soul and spirit that his mother would mold and secure.

"Niniane needed me since she was not known to Arthur and had no access to his circle of supporters. But I was the boy's closest advisor and it was my task to get Niniane within striking distance of the object of her desire.

"Poor Niniane! It was with great glee that I was able to add marital fidelity to the long list of King Ban's virtues. No flirtation, magic potion or incantation was able to influence the King to invite his passionate admirer into his bed. She begged pitifully for my help but I made sure that my own magic was not quite faultless. I was confident that my spiritual powers were imaginary but I wished to be completely innocent of complicity in Niniane's plans.

"And so she laid snares and traps for her prey for months, without success, until the last great battles were fought and Arthur's crown was sufficiently secure so that the Bretons could return to their lands across the sea.

"Niniane's efforts had failed but it was not long before she learned of Ban's travails in Brittany when he returned home. The pregnancy of his wife, Helen, and the birth of his son, Galahad, engendered new schemes in Niniane's determined brain.

"Not one to accept defeat, she realized that, though she would have had it otherwise, the gods had their own plans which never fail and she would yet have the son of Ban of Benoic that she so desperately wanted."

Merlin was never reticent in talking to me about anything and everything except about how I came into Niniane's hands. I asked him about that several times but he always managed to change the subject or tried to divert me by offering up irrelevant tidbits of gossip or politics. It required a threat, on my part, to visit him no more, before he, at last, reluctantly agreed that I would soon learn what I needed to know. What followed was a surprise I would have never suspected.

One morning, without offering any explanation, Merlin instructed me to have two horses saddled for a short ride to Watford, just northwest of Londinium. I did as he asked and we departed by mid-morning. I was fully armed but we took no squires. By mid-day we came to a prosperous looking manor and a very well appointed villa. Merlin was clearly familiar with the place and led us directly to the villa gate, which seemed to have been opened in anticipation of our arrival.

Squires and pages appeared and we were relieved of our horses. We were led to a small but comfortable and well-appointed hall where squires helped me out of my armor. Warm cider and baked confections were brought in and placed before us. Finally, a gentleman entered the room and approached. Although he appeared to have seen forty winters and was now in poor health, there was no mistaking that he had once been a knight of some prowess. He and Merlin greeted each other warmly.

"Lancelot," said Merlin, "this is Sir Mael de Tours, the son of Erwan, the Count of Tours. He was King

Ban's squire and the only witness to your father's death and your abduction by the Lady Niniane."

I had risen for the introduction but I fell back in the chair with my head spinning. I was confused and overwhelmed. Merlin pushed my head down between my knees and the floor stopped moving but not moving.

I slipped off the chair and knelt on one knee before Sir Mael.

"My lord," I said, "I am your faithful servant for all of my days."

"Rise, Sir Lancelot," he answered. "It is I who must serve you as I did your father and I shall do so by unburdening myself of the true story I have kept secret from everyone but my friend Merlin."

With that, the three of us sat knee to knee and Sir Mael began.

"You already know that your father and uncle came, with their armies, to aid Arthur in his wars after he was made King. When your father and uncle returned to Brittany they found their lands, in Benoic and Ganis, devastated by Claudas, a rich and powerful King of Frankish Gaul.

"Your mother, who was a beautiful young noblewoman named Helen, had given birth to you, her only child, while the King was still in Britain. She named you Galahad, which was your grandfather's name. Your uncle, King Bohort, was married to Evainne, Helen's sister. They had two sons named Lionel and Bors who are your closest cousins.

"King Bohort had been mortally wounded in a skirmish and, as he lay dying in his own castle in Ganis, your father's forces were besieged in the city and castle of Trebe in Benoic.

"Your father had performed so many incredible feats of valor and prowess that Claudas' knights avoided meeting him in the field at the cost of their own honor. Nevertheless, each melee cost the lives of his followers and the time finally came when there were not enough of his knights to meet the hordes sent against them in open combat. There was nothing to do then but to barricade the castle gates and wait out the siege until help came from Arthur in Britain.

"Your father never doubted that Arthur would come. The war had gone on for over a year and he was sure that the news would have reached Britain long ago. Arthur had sworn an oath to come to his and Bohort's defense. But months went by and Arthur did not come and no one from Arthur's court came to bring words of encouragement.

"Claudas finally became tired of the siege and called a truce to negotiate with your father at his war camp. He was a false king and a false knight but he was also cunning and shrewd. He made your father a tempting offer that appeared to be to his own disadvantage. Perhaps he knew or foresaw what was predestined to happen. I cannot claim to know what I do not know, but I have a right to my own conjectures. It is enough to say that just a few years after the events that I speak of now, Arthur and Claudas met with much friendliness and amity. It appeared to me as if they had been collaborators in some conspiracy.

"Claudas offered to keep the truce for forty days if your father would remain in his castle and send messengers to King Arthur, in Britain, to come to his aid as he had promised. If Arthur did come in the proscribed time, he would withdraw his army and leave your father in peace. If Arthur did not come within forty days, your father would surrender and pay homage to Claudas as his lord. Then he would have peace as Claudas' vassal.

"Your father saw no dishonor in the proposal and indeed felt it to his advantage. He agreed to the proposal and returned to your mother. When he explained everything, she agreed that there was no other choice since to refuse would mean facing defeat and enslavement.

"King Ban decided to go to Britain as his own messenger so that Arthur would not suspect trickery and delay his coming beyond the forty days. He also decided to take the Queen, and you, along with one squire. I was that squire.

"Then your father called his seneschal, who had witnessed the meeting with Claudas, and placed the safety of the castle in his hands. That night, the four of us rode secretly out of the castle and made our way into the nearby forest.

"I was told, by Sir Pharian, that the next morning the seneschal went to King Claudas and informed him that we were gone. He proposed that if the King attacked the castle, he would arrange to open the tower gates so that the King's knights could ride in without opposition and overrun the defenders. In return for this betrayal all he asked for was that Claudas make him lord of the city and castle of Trebe.

"By mid-morning, Claudas attacked the castle, and the seneschal's treason allowed his knights to fight their way in. But your father's men would not give up without a struggle, and the hopeless battle raged for hours. Finally, with death or surrender facing them, they set fire to the castle and escaped as best they could in the chaos and confusion.

"By late afternoon of the same day, we reached a small lake at the edge of the forest. As your mother rested, the King rode to the top of a high hill to look back at the castle, which he loved more than any other in his kingdom.

"He was gone a long while and your mother became concerned about his absence. She left you in my care and climbed the hill to search for him. I heard her screams and laid you, swathed in a cradle, under a tree, and ran to my Lady's rescue. When I reached the top of the hill, I saw that the King was dead and that there was nothing that I could do. When the Queen finally began to calm, I lifted the King's body onto his horse and we began the slow decent down the hill.

"When the Queen began to regain her senses, she realized that you had been left alone. She ran down the hill to where the other horses had been left. I followed as quickly as I could and as we approached the place where I had left you I saw a veiled lady standing in a small boat on the lake holding you tightly to her chest.

"I saw your mother pleading with the Lady in the boat as she moved forward, deeper and deeper into the water with her arms outstretched as if to take you back. But, the boat moved further away, out onto the lake, where a mist suddenly appeared and then the boat was gone from view.

"I buried your father facing the lake, where you disappeared, in the hope that somehow he could look after you and keep you safe. There was not much that I could do for your mother. I was a mere squire, all alone, and I could not bring her safely to my father's lands in Tours. There was an abbey nearby and that is where I took her and left her in the care of the nuns.

"When Claudas overran King Bohort's kingdom and besieged his royal castle of Montlair, Bohort was already dead. Queen Evainne disguised herself and her two young sons and escaped from the castle in fear of the fate that Claudas had in store for them. It was good fortune then, when she encountered the good Sir Pharian, who had been a loyal ally of King Bors until his death.

"Pharian and Evainne agreed that he and his wife would raise the two boys in secrecy until they were old enough to fight to recover their birthright. But Niniane interfered with that, just as she imposed her will on everything about you.

"I eventually returned to my home in Tours where I was knighted by my father. One fine day Merlin appeared and told me that the infant Galahad had survived and was in Britain. On that day I decided to leave my home, come to Britain and wait until the time that I could serve you once again."

I had finally heard everything. Merlin and I left Sir Mael with embraces and assurances of fidelity on both our parts. It was difficult to leave. I felt a strong kinship for Sir Mael who had once carried me in his arms and protected me. He had known and served my mother and my father and that made my feelings toward him more tender than any person, man or woman, I have ever known.

As we rode back to Londinium I thought back about how Niniane and Saraide steadfastly refused to tell me anything about whom I was and how I had come to be Niniane's "son". Arthur had always acted toward me as if none of his part in my father's betrayal ever happened. As I think about this tragedy I do not fault Claudas for attacking the castle. He had every right to do so, since my father had not adhered to the truce agreement by leaving and acting as his own messenger to Arthur. But, I do believe that the perfidy of my father's seneschal goes deeper than just the betrayal of the castle. The coincidence of my father's death and Niniane's appearance so close to where he died is too hard to ignore. My father was still in the prime of life. Did the seneschal have some role in my father's death? Did he know that my father would choose the hill, near the lake, where he died, to look down towards the castle? How did Niniane know where the trusted squire would leave me alone and when to appear in the lake mists to take me away?

Over the years, every time I brought up these questions Niniane looked at me with cold, angry eyes, and asked me if I had no appreciation or gratitude for all the good things she had done for me.

As I grow older, I think more and more about my father and my mother and my regret grows. If my father had not gone to Arthur's aid, I would have grown up as a king's son. Life would have been much different for me. There would be no wondering about who I was or what was expected of me. There would be the comfort of brothers and sisters. My father would have knighted me and later I would have had lands and castles. I would have been married and had children and grandchildren of my own by the age I am now.

Fate was cruel to my parents. Those my father trusted most betrayed him. His death was an insult to his memory. He deserved to die a hero's death, in battle, with a bloody sword in his hand. My mother's life was one of unceasing sorrow. To have lost, in one day, first her beloved husband, and then her only child, was a punishment that no just god would inflict.

I know that my life would have been in danger and my future would have been uncertain if Niniane had not taken me, but I can not rid myself of the guilt I share in my mother's everlasting misery. But more than that, I have a deep resentment toward Niniane for not bringing my mother to me before she died. What great harm would there have been if she had known I was alive and had one last time to hold me in her arms and kiss me?

Chapter 2

"Have you ever been to Brittany, Lonmarch?"

"No, my lord," I answered.

"Well, you should go there if you can. I have traveled there many times. It is much like Britain."

The place to which Niniane took me was an island off the southern coast of Brittany. It is separated from the mainland by a strait that is well known for its deep and treacherous currents that change wildly with the tides. For many miles east and west of the Island, most of the mainland has steep cliffs that drop almost vertically down onto rocky shoals. There are only a few sandy beaches that are wide enough to allow a small boat, from the mainland, to embark and disembark. There is no harbor on the mainland side, where even a moderately sized vessel could weigh anchor.

Anyone fortunate enough to navigate the strait then has to face a gauntlet of jagged reefs, protecting the northern side of the island, waiting to shred a boat's hull to splinters. The reefs are visible during low tide. They are hidden beneath the waves during high tide, so that is naturally the most dangerous time for passage.

To make matters worse for adventurous mariners, a mist perpetually shields the Island from the mainland, as if nature is conspiring to conceal its secrets from curious eyes.

On the southern side of the Island, out of sight of the mainland, there is one well-hidden harbor deep enough for ocean going vessels of moderate size. It is from this harbor that ships can sail west and north around Brittany to Britain or south, along the coast, to Gaul and Hispania.

With the exception of secrecy and isolation from the rest of the world, life on the Island is much like that of a small principality on the mainland. The Island has all of the main features of southern Brittany. Broad, grassy plains, green valleys, rivers, streams, freshwater ponds and lakes, high hills and forests with beech and chestnut trees. Here and there, around the Island are rugged cliffs, grassy dunes and sandy beaches.

The uncultivated lands teem with wild game. Roe deer and pheasant are hunted for food and sport. For those who are more daring, there is hunting for bear, wild boar and even wolves. The freshwater streams have trout, while the ocean waters provide salmon, turbot and shellfish. There is one manor and a few small villages on the Island as well as many small homesteads where single families or clans live and work. I suspect that the people of the Island are descendants of those who were here before the Celts. The peasants do all of the farming, animal husbandry, blacksmithing, ironwork and the rough and skilled labor necessary to maintain the manor.

Niniane had many ladies as attendants who looked to her needs and served her in every way. One of them, named Saraide was my nurse. She fed, washed and played with me and took care of me. She stayed with me until I was knighted and, even after that, she watched over me for Niniane's sake and perhaps her own.

The earliest memory I have is of me standing by a pond, throwing pebbles into the water and watching the ripples roll away from me as Saraide sat on the grass nearby. I was probably three or four years old at that time.

Niniane was my mother and, although she made

much time for me and doted on me when she could, she was involved with her affairs as master of the Island and she was often away from the Island for weeks at a time.

My childhood was a wonderful time for me. I played with other boys without regard to rank. Always rough and tumble, I was in the midst of every game and physical challenge. And being bigger and stronger than others my age, I preferred to play with those older than me. I was always chosen the leader for every prank and adventure so that when we went too far in our behavior I took the brunt of the punishment.

I was free to go where I wanted and to do what I wanted as long as I did not hurt anyone else or put myself at extreme risk. Of course, I did not know that I was never out of sight of one of Saraide's minions until I was old enough to realize that someone always instantly appeared when I was hurt and bleeding.

I was usually dirty and happy digging in the dirt, building forts and playing war games with the other boys near my age. Summer and winter, we were always throwing something at each other whether it was mud or snowballs. In winter, when it snowed enough, we slid down hills, on old, discarded shields, trying to keep from crashing into trees. But my favorite game was catching piglets. Some of us would sneak into a sty and roust up a sow with a litter. The little ones would have to stop suckling and the chase would be on. The sty was all slippery mud and it was fun to run and dive after the piglets while their mother ran after us intent on stomping us into the ground. Afterwards it was glorious fun to see the disgust on everyone's face as we paraded around, among the grown-ups, stinking of pig manure.

Usually Niniane and Saraide turned a blind eye to all of my mischief and troublemaking but they were not lax about warning me not to be cruel to any person or beast. I was not perfect and I made grievous errors of judgment and behavior but there was no need for physical punishment. I adored Niniane and Saraide and one look of disappointment from them was enough to drive me to tears of embarrassment and remorse. I would beg for forgiveness but sometimes their mercy was not quickly forthcoming and my misery was greater than the pain of any thrashing I might have had otherwise.

There was an old man named Lyvare who was always around the villa. I do not remember what he did or how he served Niniane but I do remember the stories he told about his days with King Ambrosius and King Uther of Britain. He talked about the courage and prowess of the great British knights who fought the Saxons and the Irish and the other tribes that invaded that country. He described, with much feeling, what it was like to be an honorable knight and about a knight's responsibility to help the poor and downtrodden and victims of injustice.

I think that, as young as I was, his stories about the heroes he had known and the battles he had seen made a deep impression on me and made me yearn to be a great knight and be part of the glory of knighthood. I remember that tears came to his eyes whenever he talked about the great Breton Kings, Ban and Bohort, who had helped King Arthur save his kingdom in Britain and how they had been killed through treachery.

I was told that Lyvare died when I had just been made a squire. When I think of that old man now, it is with a tender feeling of gratitude and kinship, for there is no doubt in my mind that he was, himself, once a knight of great honor and prowess and since he is in my memory, a part of him lives on in me.

Everyone knew that I was ultimately under Niniane's protection, and the older boys taunted me with the nickname of "the King's son." I could not counter their teasing because I did not know who my father was. So, the only recourse I had when the teasing became too much to bear was to fight my playmates. That is what I frequently did, one at a time or against them all at once. It did not matter much to me. In the end, the only deference paid to me was in recognition of my size, strength, prowess at games, and bearing.

My life took a great turn when, at the age of five, Niniane returned to the Island after a long time away and brought with her two boys named Lionel and Bors. They were both a bit older than I, and much more of a physical challenge for me than any of the other boys on the Island. We became very close friends and were inseparable as we found ways to get into as much mischief as we could and sharing in the punishment for misbehaving.

I had only one regret about Lionel and Bors. They knew who their father was. They were the sons of King Bohort and Queen Evianne of Ganis. They knew that their father had been killed in a war with King Claudas and that their mother had died in a nunnery. Oh, how I wished my father had been a famous king killed in a war, but no such information was ever forthcoming from Niniane or Saraide, and they did not allow my asking questions about that subject.

Our fun loving ways came to an abrupt close when I turned seven years old.

Niniane explained to Lionel, Bors and me that we

were destined to become knights when we were grown and that the time had come to begin preparing for that day. The first step was to become a page. The three of us were being sent to the court of King Gradlon. We would live and serve in his castle in Quimper on the River Odet.

I had never been off the Island before and I admit that I was nervous. Nevertheless, the voyage was a time of great adventure for the three of us. We explored every part of the vessel, except those parts we were expressly forbidden to enter. We had never been on a ship, much less sailing on the ocean. I spent hours watching the waves, looking for other ships and ocean monsters that might breach the water's surface and devour us all.

We sailed the entire first day and then through the night. Since the weather was mild, the three of us were allowed to sleep on deck. Lying on my back, watching the stars while the ship rocked and lurched on the waves was an experience of great wonder and magic, and I have never forgotten the feeling I had of peace and contentment. I remember thinking that if I had the choice, I would be a sailor and live my life on the sea and under the stars.

By mid-day of the second day, we reached an estuary on the southern coast. The captain anchored the ship and two flat-bottomed riverboats came along side. We climbed ladders down to the boats and all of our belongings were transferred to them as well. Then we waited until the tide sent the currents upstream. The men who worked the boats lowered a small sail and used long poles to push the boats up the River Odet.

My first sight of Quimper Castle astounded me. I had never seen anything so big and powerful.

Niniane's manse was nothing like this. Lionel and Bors were equally excited. They jumped and squealed whenever a new feature of the castle was revealed by our approach.

At last, our boat reached the quay where a small crowd of knights and ladies waited for us. One of the knights wore a gold circlet on his head and I assumed that he would be King Gradlon himself. I remember wondering why the king would be waiting to greet Niniane. Was she so famous or powerful that she deserved such an honor? Was she a wizard (as I had always heard rumored) who demanded such obeisance? Then it struck me that the king was taking on the responsibility for three orphan boys. Lionel and Bors were the sons of a king, but who was I?

Then, the time for thinking was over and we were caught up in the excitement of King Gradlon's welcome.

For three days, we were free to explore the castle, and the grounds surrounding it, without restriction or supervision. The stables, with its giant chargers, the armory with its swords and lances and every other weapon imaginable, the iron working forges and especially the huge enclosed courts where the knights and squires practiced their fighting skills, all held extreme fascination for us. Then, on the fourth day, we were summoned to the King's chambers where Niniane and Saraide were waiting for us.

"My dears," Niniane said, "it is time for me to return to the Island and for you to begin your training for knighthood. In all things, King Gradlon is your liege lord and master. You will obey him as you have obeyed me. Your training will be hard, but that is as it should be. You are destined to be knights of great honor and prowess.

"Saraide will remain here with you, but she will not guide or protect you. She stays here for my sake.

"I leave here today. Tomorrow you begin your training."

With the end of her speech, Niniane hugged Lionel and Bors and kissed their cheeks. But then she hugged me and kissed my lips and eyes and cheeks and would not let go of me.

In that instant, the love I had for Niniane came welling up in me and I held tight and buried my head in her breast. I did not want to let her go. I could not bear to have my mother leave me.

Finally, King Gradlon came over to us. He put his hand on my shoulder and said, "It is time to show the courage you must have to be a great knight, young Lancelot. Come with me. It is time to meet your tutor."

With a firm grip, the King drew me away from Niniane. He turned me from her, and when I turned back, she was gone.

Chapter 3

That night, I slept in the castle in a large room with six beds: for Lionel and Bors, and me and three other boys named de Vertain, Clarius and Dinard, whose fathers were noblemen. We were to be companions for the next ten years and shared all of the trials and tribulations of training for knighthood. For all of the hard and constant work, I look back on those years as the happiest and most carefree of my life. In the end, I was the only one of us who was not made a knight by King Gradlon.

The next morning, we were brought before the King and a tall, handsome knight of middle age named Sir de Touars. He was to be our unchallenged lord and master in all things. We would be his pages, and later his squires, until we were either ready for knighthood or dismal failures to be returned to our homes in dishonor. Sir de Touars was not one for delay, and we began to learn our duties as soon as we were dismissed from the King's presence.

There was far more to preparing for knighthood than learning how to fight. As a page I received a good education. The castle priest was the tutor, and he taught me how to read and write in the British language. Because I learned easily, he also taught me a bit of Latin and enough about numbers so that I could to do sums. The priest was also responsible for teaching me about the new religion, including the holidays and saints and prayers to be made at special times. He tried hard, but I could not understand the god that had three parts. There was the Lord, the son of the Lord and the spirit of the Lord. In any case, I learned far more about the old religion from the boys in the town, and those gods were much easier to understand since it was simple to know what they wanted and how to pray to them.

Along with Bors and Lionel and the other boys, I spent part of each day riding ponies and fighting in pairs with wooden swords both on foot and mounted. A metal ring was hung on a string attached to the arm of a post. We were drilled over and over again until we could pass a lance through the ring while riding the pony at full gallop. After that we learned to joust against the quintain. I received many a swift and painful swipe in the rear because I did not get out of the way of the mace in time.

Sir de Touars made these exercises seem like fun and games at first, but as we improved our skills, he became more serious about correcting or reproaching us.

While we were learning knightly skills, we were also given tasks intended to build our strength and stamina. From digging latrines to running alongside a trotting horse to carrying quarry stones for buildings and walls, we did what was demanded of us to improve our bodies as much as it was possible to do.

I was never punished or treated cruelly. Nevertheless, more was demanded of me than anyone else. Perhaps it was because I was the strongest and had the most stamina of all the pages anywhere near my age. I seemed to challenge my tutors to find the limits of my strength and ability, without doing me serious harm or injury, since I would not give up and ask for rest or relief.

We also learned how to hunt for wild game including tracking, killing and dressing our quarry. At first, we hunted deer and used dogs to hunt for rabbits and other ground game, as well as birds. Later, as we became more proficient, we hunted fox and lynx. All of our kills were made with the bow and arrows. It was not until we were squires and capable with the spear and lance, that we were included in hunts for wolves, wild boar and bears.

We hunted in small groups led by an experienced forester. Part of the lesson was to hunt together and rely on each other while gaining real experience in using our weapons and practicing our riding skills in rough and wooded terrain.

When I was twelve years old, my service as a page ended and I became a squire. It was with joy and trepidation that I received my new title.

As a page, carrying out errands, serving food and performing services at mealtimes and feasts, I had watched how the knights, squires and other noblemen behaved towards the ladies of the court. I watched their courtly manners and heard their courtly speech. I saw how they dressed and preened themselves and danced and played games. I felt that all of that was unmanly, and I wanted none of it. But, as a squire it was my duty to learn all of that foppishness, and whether I wanted to or not, I did as required.

Off to one side of the stables was the "behourd," enclosed by a palisade wall with one large door. I spent hours there, every day, practicing with the other pages, as well as squires and knights, to develop and improve our skills with weapons and to build strength and stamina. In the center of the field was the "Pell". It was as big around as my waist and carved from a tree trunk then buried, end down, several feet into the ground. Using wooden swords, much heavier than real swords, we beat on that Pell for hours and practiced thrusting, cutting, and slicing. We also practiced beating on it with a shield and striking it with the sword hilt. In short, we practiced every maneuver and every weapon on the Pell that we were likely to use in real combat. The real advantage to the Pell was that we did not hurt anyone else and the Pell, of course, did not hit back. Nevertheless, all of us took to working hard at the Pell, realizing that it was the key to building our skills, strength and agility.

Sir de Touars had been my master since the beginning, and it was with great relief and joy that he accepted me as his youngest squire. I was more than pleased, as Sir de Touars was an exceptionally active and adventurous knight. He did not like courtly life and preferred tournaments and jousting. Without any warning, he was likely to tell Baldwin and Arnulf, who were young, newly made knights, and me, to pack for an adventure in some distant country.

Under Sir de Touars' tutelage, I learned about armor and how to prepare for battle. I took care of his weapons, especially his sword, and made sure that his horses, especially his courser, were fed, brushed and combed and kept in good health and prepared for battle.

Tournaments were exciting with all of their color, waving flags and pennants and the sounds of clashing arms and blaring trumpets. If Sir de Touras shattered a lance or broke a sword in the lists, I would rush to him with a replacement. If he was in a melee, I would have to duck and dodge to avoid being crushed by the giant horses or beheaded by a flashing blade. To me that was the height of adventure, and I looked forward to those opportunities, even if they were at Sir de Touars' expense.

In spite of my youth, my size, strength, daring and skills on a horse and with weapons could not be ignored. Sir de Touras challenged me in mock combat at every opportunity. We jousted with blunted lances and fought man to boy with wrapped swords for hours, with neither one of us holding back one bit. Under his watchful eye, Baldwin and Arnulf would attack me together with whatever weapons they chose, and I would have to defend myself without a shield.

I understood much later, when I was old enough to think about such things, that Sir de Touras, Baldwin and Arnulf had formed a pact to exert themselves on my behalf. They were helping me develop my skills and strength. They did everything they could to make me what I was capable of being. They sacrificed their own interests to advance mine.

There have been many moments over the past few years when I have thought about Sir de Touras and my two companions, and how much I have to thank them for what prowess I possess. I wonder if they think of me and if they have heard anything about me. Have they heard that I was indeed as noble born as they and not some bastard cast-off? I wonder if I returned to Brittany to claim my inheritance would they be friend or foe?

By the time I was sixteen years old there was no knight in King Gradlon's court who could overcome me in any joust or hand to hand combat. There was no one who could best me in horsemanship, archery or any athletic skill such as running, wrestling, jumping or throwing the javelin or hammer.

One day, after a particularly hard practice, Sir de Touars called me to him and asked that I walk with him to the castle garden. I was apprehensive, to say the least, but his calm manner reassured me that I was not in any very great trouble. When we were well out of sight and hearing of anyone else he stopped and faced me.

"Lancelot," he said, " you are unlike any squire I have ever met and I wager that you will be unlike any knight you will ever encounter. You seem to be two different squires in the same body. In all of your affairs you are calm and thoughtful. Your courtesy, grace, manners and bearing are noble and your behavior towards the young maids and damsels is beyond reproach, in spite of their obvious affectionate intentions toward you. Yet, in the lists or in combat with your brothers, you are as if possessed by demons. There is no expression of anger or fear on your face when you fight. You attack your opponent as if the fate of Brittany was in your hands. You appear to be driven by some inward rage and charge with a wild frenzy, but you never seem to abandon your skills and control of your weapons. When you oppose your brothers I fear for their safety but you never do them grievous harm even though I know that you can.

"You are younger than Bors and Lionel but you are superior to them in size, strength and prowess. Because of everything I have just told you I have proposed to the King that he send for Dame Niniane to discuss the knighting of the three of you."

I was stunned by what Sir de Touars said but the full comprehension of what I heard was not long in coming. I grabbed his hand and shook it wildly while I babbled my undying respect, love and appreciation. Then, as soon as he rescued his hand and gave me his permission I was off at a run to tell Lionel and Bors the good news.

It was later that night, as I laid awake in my bed reliving Sir de Touars' words, that a great weight of guilt came over me. He praised me for my restraint towards the ladies of the court but he knew nothing about what I had been doing with the ladies of the town. When I was a mere thirteen summers the older squires took me to a street in the town where men could lay with women. From that time on, I thought about naked women almost all the time and whenever I had the silver coins, and I could sneak away from the castle, I went to that street.

But what I was doing could not have been dishonorable. All of the squires, except for Bors, did the same thing and the women of the town were not pure and innocent as were the noble maids and damsels of the court. Neither Niniane nor Saraide had ever talked to me about this and I could not imagine what harm there was in anything so pleasurable. Still, I had an uneasy feeling that what I was doing was somehow unacceptable. I decided that, nevertheless, Sir de Touars' judgment of me was deserved and I vowed, to myself, never to use town women again. With my guilt assuaged, I fell soundly asleep.

One day King Gradlon appeared at the behourd. Sir de Touras and the King watched me at my exercises for a while and whispered to themselves. I sensed that something was about to change in my life and I hoped that it would be for the best. Then, about one week later, a page came and summoned me to the King's chambers. I straightened my hair and my tunic and followed the boy. When I entered the King's room the first thing I saw was my Lady Niniane smiling at me but with the look of great surprise on her face.

It was a tearful and joyous reunion. We had not seen each other for ten years and, while she had not changed much, I had grown from a boy to an almost full-grown man. But at the sight of Niniane, I was a child again, and I hugged and kissed her as a happy child who has missed his long lost mother.

Finally, she pushed me away and held me at arm's length.

"My son," she said, with a very determined and serious look on her face, "what do you hope to do with your life?"

"My lady," I answered, "I hope to be a knight."

"Ah, my son, if you knew what difficulties and travails a true knight must bear, you might not be so anxious to follow that path. Whoever wishes to be a knight must accept a life of toil. He who seeks wealth, comfort, safety and ease in life cannot be a true knight."

"My lady, a man would be a coward or a fool to turn away from the opportunity to be a knight."

"Let me tell you," said Niniane, "what I know of knighthood so that you can consider your decision with reason and understanding. Avarice and cruelty have always existed in this world. Strength and power have always been able to overcome justice. The weak could not defend themselves against the strong. Long ago the people decided to choose the most worthy and the bravest young men to protect the peaceful folk and to defend their rights against those who were beyond the law. Those warriors were the powerful and courageous men who fought against evil and defended the innocent. They were the first knights. A knight who is true to the code of knighthood must be courteous without being corrupt, gracious without being cruel, compassionate toward the needy, generous and prepared to help those in need.

"A knight should be a fair judge, without love or hate, in defending the right against the wrong. Knightly honor is loyalty to one's lord, loyalty to fellow knights, accepting an opponent's surrender, not attacking an opponent's horse, waiting for an opponent to be armed and ready and not attacking those too weak to defend themselves.

"A knight should never do anything dishonorable or shameful to save his own life. A true knight should prefer his own death to dishonor.

"A true knight should oppose those who are treacherous, cruel, evil and unjust yet be gracious and compassionate to those who are good and in need of help or rescue.

"A true knight must accept every danger and every battle to serve his liege lord and the people who rely upon him even at the risk of his own death or maiming. He must accept cold, hunger and loneliness and turn away from the comforts of warm hearths and soft women. He must earn his daily meal and his night's lodging by the strength of his body and the courage of his heart. He must avoid the thoughts and company of all women since they will destroy a true knight's purity and lead to his fall from grace and honor and they will weaken him and bring about his loss of prowess.

"Now, my dear son, do you still wish to be a knight?"

"With all my heart, dear Lady."

"My dear, King Gradlon has consented to knight Lionel and Bors. When I have finished preparing all that is necessary, I will take you to the country of Britain where Arthur is king. The greatest knights in the world sit at Arthur's table and you will gain much fame and honor in that land. In time, you will be the most precious, most courtly, the bravest, the one richest in good qualities, and the most worthy man who ever had the title of knight.

"Prepare yourself. Your wish will be fulfilled. We travel to Britain. You will be knighted by none other than King Arthur."

Our farewells were a mixture of sadness, regret, excitement and joy. King Gradlon and Sir de Touars had been our lords, tutors and friends for so many years. Lionel, Bors and I had grown as close as brothers to the other squires and young pages and especially to the other young knights who had just received the accolade with Lionel and Bors. Our parting would be especially hard on King Gradlon's Queen who had looked after me like a mother in spite of Saraide's presence.

Nevertheless, the time came for me to leave Quimper Castle for the last time. I wondered if I would ever return and, if I did, would the people I had come to love and respect still be here. With one long last sigh I whispered, "Good-bye."

Our small party rode at a moderate pace out of the castle, through the town and down to the river. There were just seven of us: Niniane and two of her squires, Saraide, Lionel, Bors and me. We took no weapons, armor, clothing or possessions of any kind. When we reached the quay on the river, we left the palfreys with a farrier and boarded a small boat manned by several watermen who untied the hawsers and deployed a sail as soon as we were free of land.

Ahead of us was a large sea-going vessel with two tall masts and many sails. I was no longer a child and the sight of that impressively large ship did not excite me, as it would have when I was a boy. Still, I was excited and anxious to be on board and under way.

When the boat was secured safely to the ship, Lionel, Bors and I clambered up rope ladders to the deck. Niniane and Saraide were lifted up in ship's chairs attached to ropes and pulleys. Almost as soon as we were on board, the ship's master ordered the anchor raised and the sails set. The wind was favorable and soon we were slashing through the water, west by southwest, away from the southern coast of Brittany.

We sailed for ten days; first around the jagged coast of west Brittany, then north and east through the great open sea between Gaul and Britain. The master kept his course close to the Gaulish coast until we passed through narrow straits and saw the white chalk cliffs on the western shore. This was the sign for the ship to cleave to the British coastline, and it was not long before we dropped anchor and made landfall near the town of Ramsgate, not far from Canterbury.

Chapter 4

When we disembarked, there were two squires waiting with palfreys for all of us. After we regained our land legs, we mounted and rode off, following the squires.

After a short ride, we came to an encampment filled with pavilions and people. Once again, I was amazed by Niniane's powers to arrange things as she wished. There were knights, squires, pages, ladies and attendants of all sorts. Although they were out of sight, I could smell horses and hear an occasional whinny. Niniane had ordered this small settlement to be built for our privacy and comfort. People were busy, rushing about and performing their assigned tasks, but Lionel, Bors and I were not allowed to wander around or talk to anyone except Niniane or Saraide. The three of us ate, drank and slept that night in one pavilion, which we were prohibited from leaving.

The next morning was one I shall never forget. When we were called from our pavilion, we were presented with our armor, weapons and horses.

Nothing in my life had prepared me for what was brought before me. Three squires came forward holding my shield, lance, and hauberk. The shield and lance were gleaming white. The hauberk was silver. Another squire held my helmet made of hammered silver and gold. A page held a white cape trimmed with ermine and encrusted with jewels and precious gems. Finally, a knight approached holding my sword made of the strongest metal and a scabbard made of gold and covered with jewels.

I was overwhelmed by the richness of these gifts from Niniane, and then a saddled horse was brought forward. I heard nothing and saw nothing else after that and I thought that my legs would fail and I would drop to my knees.

I had never seen a destrier such as this one, nor had I ever dreamed that one such as he existed. As white as snow, without a single blemish, he was taller and more massive than I could have imagined. He had powerfully muscled shoulders, legs, and an enormous chest. His coat glistened, his nostrils flared, and as he pawed the ground with impatience, I could feel the earth tremble. This would be the steed to carry me to honor and glory if only I had the strength, courage and the prowess to match his.

I took the reins from the squire who held him and patted the destrier's neck and cheek. I rubbed his forehead and he quieted down and sniffed me. I reached up to scratch his ear and, as he bowed his fine head, I whispered to him, "You are Fer de Blanc and where we ride together, my life and honor will be yours to keep."

I leaped into the saddle and, even before I was settled, he began to gallop through the encampment. I could feel the power under me, and I started to laugh with the great joy I felt. The sound of his pounding hooves echoed throughout my body. He seemed to glide over the ground and his gait, even at the gallop, suited me perfectly. I knew that he and I were as one. It took all the will I had to rein him in and return to Niniane and the crowd of cheering people I had left behind.

Later that morning, Niniane ordered that the three of us be dressed and armored, and that all of her knights and ladies make their preparations for travel as well. When all was done to her satisfaction, we were told to mount our horses and follow where she led. The procession was magnificent. First, came Niniane, dressed and veiled all in white, riding a perfect white palfrey. Following her were three ladies, similarly dressed in white and mounted on white palfreys. Lionel, Bors and I, wearing our new armor and our bejeweled capes and riding our magnificent and richly saddled destrier's, followed next, Lionel on his black and Bors on his chestnut. Then came Saraide. And, finally, forty heavily armed knights followed us.

On that day, King Arthur was in Canterbury with most of his court, including the Queen. In the morning, he left his lodgings with some of his companions to hunt in the nearby woods. Toward evening, as they were returning, the King and his party were surprised and delighted when they encountered our entourage at a crossroad. Niniane, with Lionel, Bors and me beside her, rode up to the King and saluted him. The King returned the salute and asked what her purpose was in being on that road.

"My lord," Niniane said, "I come to offer you two gifts and ask for one gift in return. I assure you that all three will bring you great honor."

Arthur, who recognized wealth and power when he saw it, was suitably impressed by the richness and size of Niniane's train.

"Lady," he said, "even if it should cost me a great deal, you shall have what you ask."

Niniane motioned for Lionel and Bors to come forward.

"My lord," said Niniane, "I ask that you accept these two, young, newly made knights into your household."

"Lady, that I will gladly do if you tell me their names and who knighted them."

"Their names are Sir Lionel and Sir Bors and they were knighted by King Gradlon of Brittany who knows their parentage. I cannot tell you now who their parents were, but King Gradlon is well known to you and you know that he would not have knighted them without being sure of their nobility and their prowess."

"Now as to this third young man," she said, pointing to me, "he has not yet been knighted and I ask that you perform the accolade when he requests it."

"Lady," replied the King, "I shall gladly welcome Sir Lionel and Sir Bors to my court, but as for this young man, first you must tell me his name, and the name of his father and mother, or give me assurances of his nobility."

Niniane moved her horse next to the King and leaned over toward him so that no one else could hear her response.

"The name I have given him is Lancelot. I will tell you no more except for my name. I am called the Lady of the Lake. We have met each other before. I have come to claim the gift you promised me, when you came to me with Merlin, and I gave you the sword Excalibur."

The King looked shocked at these words, for he had not recognized Niniane as the lady who had given him his most prized possession. For an instant it seemed as if Arthur might refuse the request, since knighting a squire who was not noble could not be tolerated. But then, he must have thought of the likelihood that Merlin had contrived this arrangement.

"My lady," said Arthur, when he could finally speak, "you shall have what you have asked for, since I have no doubt that this young man whom you bring to me is as noble as my sword."

With that assurance, Niniane thanked the King and rode away a short distance with me beside her.

After we dismounted, she turned to me and said, "My dear, you must demand to be knighted by the King no more than one day after arriving at his court. Once you are knighted, you must not stay one more night at court. You must leave immediately with your squires and seek adventures. Travel throughout the land and across all countries without seeking rest or comfort. Make no friendships that would hold you in one place. You must face the most terrible and dangerous adventures with courage and confidence. Remember, my dearest, what I have taught you about the burdens and nobility of knighthood. And, above all, in all that you do, you must have a fine and pure heart. You must never soil your holy body and spirit with courtesans or paramours."

A chill went through my body as I pictured my youthful indiscretions, but what was done was done and I forced those memories aside. I tried to change the subject.

"My lady," I asked, "why will you not tell King Arthur who I am and of my lineage?"

"My dear son, if Arthur and his court knew who you are and your father's name, you would be treated with great honor and deference, for his name is well known and revered by all good knights. You would be given gifts and comforts, which you have not earned in your own right through prowess and chivalry.

"Honor should not be lightly given. It should be earned. That is why you must not remain in Arthur's court. As soon as you are knighted, you must leave the court with your squires to seek adventures everywhere and fight every honorable battle that may come your way.

"Your name and lineage will be known to you and the world in good time. You must win your honor and prove your courage before that happens. Let no man say that your place at Arthur's side was given as payment for a debt."

"My lady, your instructions are sufficient for me, and your explanation gives me great happiness. I will do exactly as you require of me because of my love for you. I will seek adventures and battles, and I will learn what kind of man I am. I will see if I have the strength and courage to earn my own honor and deserve my father's name."

"Lancelot, my dearest, I have watched you grow since your infancy, and there is no doubt that you are the true son of a great man. Now is the time for you to go into the world and make your mark for all time. I have one last gift for you. Three squires will attend you. They are the sons of noble fathers and they have the strength, courage, loyalty and wisdom to serve you well. When their time comes, you will knight them with pride and gratitude."

Then, the Lady Niniane embraced me. I held her closely, without saying a word. She finally pushed herself away and walked slowly towards Lionel and Bors. They quickly dismounted and rushed to her. How sorrowful was their parting, for they loved her as much as I did, and her love for them almost matched her love for me. At last, Niniane walked towards her palfrey. A squire helped her mount, and she slowly rode away without a single glance backward. Bors, Lionel, and I watched the Lady until we could see her no more. All the others in her train, who had witnessed this sad parting, followed the Lady, deep in their own sorrowful thoughts.

I was heartbroken at parting from Niniane, but I was reassured by what she had told me about my father. A young man's broken heart is quick to mend and by the time Niniane was out of sight I was already thinking about my squires, the future and the adventures ahead of me. When I rode back to where the King waited, Arthur turned to his companion, Sir Yvain, and said, "I am placing this young squire in your care. I can think of no one better than you to teach him how to conduct himself."

Then, we all turned our horses toward Canterbury.

When we arrived, Lionel and Bors were taken to lodge with two of Arthur's knights, while Yvain took me to his own lodgings, where I was fed and put comfortably to bed.

The next morning, I went to Yvain and said, "My lord, the King promised my lady to make me a knight whenever I asked. I wish to be knighted tomorrow."

Yvain was surprised by the suddenness of my request, but he went to the King and told him what I had demanded. The King was at his morning meal with Queen Guinevere and his nephew, the great Sir Gawain.

Yvain later told me that when Arthur was told of my demand he was reluctant to be hurried and sought agreement that my knighting be postponed.

"Gawaine," he said, "that young man already wishes to be knighted. It is too soon. We hardly know him, and many preparations will have to be made. What do you think of that?"

"That is what you promised his lady, my lord," answered Gawaine.

"Who is this young man you are talking about?" asked Guinevere.

"We only know that his name is Lancelot, and that he was brought to us by the Lady of the Lake. But he is the handsomest, most well-built young man I have ever seen," answered Yvain.

Guinevere's curiosity was aroused and she wanted to see me. So, Yvain returned to his lodgings and had me dressed in the finest and richest clothes I had brought with me. Then he took me back to the hall where the King and Queen waited with Gawaine.

The Queen was only three years older than me, but she was a married woman and worldly wise. She stared at me, but I held my head down and could only briefly glance at her. I had never seen anyone so beautiful. I trembled so much with nervousness and excitement that I could barely mumble a salutation.

"Who are his parents?" Guinevere asked.

"We do not know," answered Yvain.

"Where does he come from?" she asked.

"We do not know, my lady, but his accent and manner of speech are like those who come from Brittany."

The Queen reached out and took my hand to question me further. But I shook so visibly at her touch that she let go of me, not wanting to embarrass me further. She signaled that the interview was over, and Yvain took me back to his lodgings, where I kept thinking about my lack of courtliness and abysmal behavior.

King Gradlon had knighted Lionel and Bors by tying on their spurs and clapping them on each shoulder with their swords. I was not to be so fortunate. Arthur's acceptance of the new religion was complete, and he vigorously adopted all of the rituals and ceremonies of the Christ church. My knighting ceremony had to follow the new religion's way to assure my devotion to their god, their priests and their chapels.

The ritual started that night under Yvain's orders. First, I was stripped bare, washed, and scrubbed head to toe by attendants. This was a symbol of my purification from sin. Then I was dressed in white vesture, for purity, and a red robe, for nobility, and marched to the Canterbury chapel.

My sword, shield and spurs had been placed on the altar, and I was left alone with them for the rest of the night. I knew that I was supposed to kneel and pray for all of that time, but I was not about to perform such a ridiculous and meaningless devotion. If a prayer could not be answered in as much time as it took to utter it why would it be answered if I uttered it over and over again all night long?

Finally, morning came and the chapel doors opened. Arthur, Yvain, Gawain, Lionel, Bors and many more knights and ladies crowded into the chapel to hear a priest say prayers and drone on about the duties of a knight. Then he blessed my sword. When he was finished, Yvain took my shield, sword and spurs from the altar and handed them to Arthur. Gawain took my arm and led me to the King. Then he pushed down on my shoulder to remind me to kneel.

I had practiced with Yvain and was able to swear an oath of allegiance and fealty to the King and to swear several other oaths. Then Arthur swatted me on both shoulders with the flat of my sword and said, loud enough for all to hear, "Lancelot of the Lake, I dub thee Sir Knight."

As soon as Yvain and Gawain tied on my spurs, belted on my sword and hung my shield around my neck, I heard Lionel and Bors start to cheer and whistle. Then the crowd broke out into "huzza's" and the congratulations and slaps on the back continued until almost everyone left the chapel.

Yvain and Gawain were almost gleeful, and I thought to myself that if they are so happy, they must have known something I did not.

As we walked out into the sunshine from that dark and musty chapel, Yvain took my arm and said, "Well, Sir Knight, it is now your duty to dress in your finest clothes and attend the feast and celebration of your rebirth."

The mid-day meal had been hurriedly turned into a feast in honor of my knighting. The great hall of Canterbury was crowded with the King, Queen, many knights, and their ladies. I was seated in a place of honor opposite the King. But before the first salvers of food were brought in, an armed knight came into the hall and approached the King.

"King Arthur," said the knight, "My name is Sir Tisant, and I have come on behalf of the Lady of Nohaut. The King of Northumberland is waging war on her and has besieged her in her castle. He has killed many of her people and laid waste to her lands. The king falsely accuses my lady of not fulfilling an agreement. He has offered to settle the dispute by armed combat, and has challenged her to choose a knight to defend her rights. My lady has no one who can match the King's best knights, and has sent me to you to beg for a champion to defend her honor and her rights in single combat."

"Sir Tisant," said Arthur, "the Lady of Nohaut is indeed my well-loved liege woman and be assured that I shall help her without fail."

Everyone had heard the knight's request and Arthur's answer. Before anyone else could say a word, I leaped from my seat.

"My lord," I shouted, "you have knighted me by your own hand and now I ask that you permit me to go to the assistance of this knight's lady as he has requested."

"Young man," said Arthur, "the King of Northumberland has many knights of great prowess and experience at battles. I fear that you are not ready to take on such a great challenge."

"My lord," I replied, "I am a knight and this is a proper request I have made of you. Do not dishonor me by refusing what is honorable for me to ask."

Sir Gawaine leaned close to the King and said, quietly so that others would not hear, "My lord, grant this young man his request. You cannot refuse him with honor, and he may well succeed. Besides, if he fails, we can find other ways to assist the lady."

Arthur reluctantly agreed, and the next morning my squires, Cael, Brandon and Loegaire, Sir Tisant and I completed our preparations for the journey to Nohaut.

When I was almost fully armed, I turned to Sir Yvain and said, "My lord, I must not go until I take my leave of my lady, the Queen."

Yvain was more than a bit surprised since my previous audience with the Queen had been so difficult, if not embarrassing, for me. Besides, it was presumptuous for a newly made knight of unproven valor and unknown parentage to seek such an audience with the highest royalty. Nevertheless, Yvain agreed to escort me to the Queen's chambers, and when I saw her, I approached with newfound and surprising confidence and knelt at her feet.

"My lady," said Yvain, "this young man wishes to bid you farewell."

The Queen had seen me knighted and had witnessed my demand for the adventure on behalf of the Lady of Nohaut. She recognized me at once.

"My dear friend," the Queen said, "I fear for you since you are so young to be going on such an adventure."

"Nevertheless," I said with my eyes cast down, "I beg you, with all my heart, to consider me your knight."

"Certainly, dear friend," she answered, and she took my hand and raised me up from my knees.

Yvain touched my arm, and I knew this meeting was over. I was in a state of confusion and disappointment as I left the Queen. The meeting had been so brief. She had called me "dear friend," but she seemed distant and not truly interested in me. But then, what more could she have said or done. She was the Queen and no one really knew who I was. It would not have been proper for her to embrace a knight of low birth. I tried to take comfort in Niniane's assurance that I was truly born of noble blood, and that someday, the Queen would have no concern about embracing me.

We returned to Yvain's lodging and I completed arming myself. When I was ready, I embraced Yvain and he wished me well. Lionel and Bors had come to see me off and we hugged and kissed each other. Then I mounted my great white horse and rode out of Canterbury, with my four companions, towards my first adventure, known only as Lancelot of the Lake.

Chapter 5

The day was sunny and bright as we rode for a while down a road through the forest until saw, a short distance away, a very fine pavilion set in an open field near a stream.

"Sir Tisant," I asked, "do you know anything about that pavilion?"

"Yes, sir," he answered, "a beautiful damsel is in that pavilion. She is guarded by a knight who is much taller and much stronger than any knight I have ever seen. He has a great hatred for King Arthur and he waits here, on the road from Londinium, so that he may encounter and kill or maim the King's knights. He has defeated every knight he has ever fought, and he is extremely cruel after he has beaten them."

"I wish to meet this knight. Wait here for me by the stream."

I rode toward the pavilion with my sword in my hand and my squires behind me. As I approached, I saw the tall knight, dressed in a long tunic and leggings, sitting in a chair near the pavilion entrance.

"Go away," shouted the knight gruffly, "you have no business here."

"Yes, I have. I wish to see the damsel who is inside the pavilion."

I rode closer to the pavilion and was about to dismount and enter, when the knight stood up, grabbed my horse's bridle and blocked my path. The knight who stood before me was at least thirty years old and the veteran of many battles, some of which were recorded by the scars on his hands, arms and face. He was a full head taller than me and even broader than me in the shoulders and chest.

"Stop, sir," he said. "The damsel is sleeping, and I do not want anyone to wake her up. I shall not fight to stop you, since I would gain no honor in killing you because you are so young and I am much bigger and stronger than you. But I will allow you to see her when she awakens."

"Why you will not fight me is of no concern" I answered, "but you must promise to show me the damsel when she wakens."

"I so promise," replied the knight. "If you return tomorrow, perhaps you can see my lady then."

At that remark, I felt the blood rush to my head and I thought that it would burst out of me. My hands clenched into fists and the nails dug into my palms. With a vicious pull on the reins, I turned my horse's head and galloped across the clearing, followed by my squires.

When we were well clear of the pavilion, I turned to look at my squires. I expected to see relief on their faces, but what I saw instead was horror. Then, in an instant of clarity, I understood what I had done. I had shown cowardice by retreating from a fight in fear for my life and safety. I felt as if I had been struck with an axe. I was ashamed. It was a feeling I had never known before. I seethed with hatred for myself. I wheeled my horse around and galloped back to the pavilion.

My horse slid to a halt in front of the pavilion, and the tall knight rose from where he was sitting and came toward me.

"I have come to see the Lady now," I shouted. "I will not wait until tomorrow."

He sneered at me and said that he would not let me see her without a fight.

There was no going back now. Trying my best to sound light-hearted and confident, I told him to arm himself quickly, since I had important business elsewhere.

He laughed at me. He said that I wasn't worth the bother of putting on his armor. He called me a puny youth, and bragged that he would make short work of me dressed as he was.

He leaped onto his horse and grabbed a shield and lance from his page, who had been watching and was ready.

He had demeaned and belittled me. My forehead pounded and I hated him as I had never hated anyone. I was in a rage. I wanted to kill him.

We each rode to the opposite ends of the clear space surrounding the pavilion and charged full tilt with our lances at the ready.

The knight struck the center of my shield so hard that it splintered and pieces went flying into the air.

My lance struck with greater force. I also hit the center of his shield, but the shield held together and drove into his left side. The force of the blow was enough to lift the knight out of his saddle and throw him to the ground.

My anger and hate were gone in an instant. I dismounted quickly and ran to the knight concerned that he was dead, but though he was badly wounded and bleeding, I was sure that I had not given him a mortal blow.

The knight's page had also run to assist his lord, and as I watched, he cradled the knight's head in his lap and administered something that caused the knight to regain consciousness.

He looked at me, took a shallow but painful breath and wheezed. “Now you may see my lady. I give her up to you and curse the day I ever saw you.”

I walked to the pavilion, which was unattended, and went inside.

The knight’s lady was standing. She was young, but older than I was. She was beautiful, as Sir Tisant had said. Her long black hair was draped over her bare shoulders and in front of her breasts, which were bare. She looked past me, her eyes steady and unblinking, as if I was not really there. I stared back at her, unable to look away, and felt my heart pounding harder than when I had faced her lord’s lance. I trembled with excitement at the thought that I had won her, that she belonged to me and I could do with her as I wished. I wanted to touch her and kiss her and then carry her to the bed behind her but I could not bring myself to move. Finally, with Niniane’s warning screaming in my brain, I turned without a word and left her where she stood.

I returned to where the knight was still laying. “Sir,” I said, “she cannot be mine. Though I have won her, I cannot be responsible for her.”

The knight was confused. “Sir, since you will not take her, tell me what to do with her.”

“When you have recovered, and can travel, take her to King Arthur’s court and tell my lady, the Queen, that the young knight, who has gone to the aid of the Lady of Nohaut, sends this damsel to her. Then take yourself to Sir Yvain, and tell him that I have sent you to him to be his vassal.”

“Sir,” said the knight, “I will do as you wish.”

With that assurance, there was nothing more for me to say or do, and I rode away with my squires behind me.

As my horse ambled slowly down a dim path, it came to me that the battle had taken only as long as it took for the horses to come together. Was I a knight of incredible prowess, or had a power greater than me guided my lance and kept me in the saddle?

I was still excited and full of nervous energy. I wanted someone to talk with about the battle. Even though Bors and Lionel were simple, they would have understood what I had done. They would have congratulated and celebrated with me. After all, at sixteen, I was already a conquering hero. But, no one knew about the battle, and I had no one to talk to.

As we continued riding slowly toward Nohaut, my thoughts became more disturbing and confused. When we reached a pleasant tree-shaded glade, I gave the signal to dismount, and I ordered Cael to help me out of my armor and have the horses attended to.

A small stream was nearby and I wandered down an embankment to ponder the water rushing over and between the smooth rocks. Just a bit downstream was a small pool of quiet water. Would I be like that stream, behaving every which way without rules and constancy? I had behaved like the boy that I was, making unreasonable demands of a man for no good reason. If I really wanted to fight that knight, why didn't I just challenge him, instead of demanding to see his lady? Was I more interested in the lady than I was in honorable combat?

Did I turn away from that knight the first time because my sense of honor bothered me or because I was afraid? I shivered at the thought that I might have been afraid at first. As I stared at the rocks in the stream, Niniane's reassuring words came back to me. She had admonished me "to be courageous, to fight and not fear defeat."

Those were just words to Niniane. But now, having fought my first real battle, I understood the meaning of fear and courage. They are the two sides of the same coin. There can be no courage without fear. To fight blindly, without fear, is no act of courage and killing without a care is dishonorable. But to overcome fear is the great test of courage. Now I felt in my heart that fear would never stop me from facing death or injury. My courage would never fail me no matter how grave or terrible the challenge that faced me.

Then I realized that I had not done too badly after all. I was barely sixteen years old. I had faced a knight bigger and stronger than I. He was the winner of many jousts and battles against Arthur's knights. I had never been in a real fight before. This was the first time. I could have been killed or maimed for life. This was no longer training. This had been a real battle, and I was the victor.

I turned abruptly away from the stream and walked quickly back toward the horses. I had my armor put back on, the horses were saddled, and we continued on our way toward Nohaut.

"Damn the past," I said to myself. "Now is the time to test my strength and prowess. I have courage enough to prove my worth."

Chapter 6

As we came up to the top of a steep hill, I could see all of Nohaut in the very broad valley and the lower hills below me. Farms and cultivated fields were everywhere. The richness of the land was evident from the number of buildings, the green pastures in which I could see large numbers of grazing cattle, and the fair town surrounding a large palace.

The Lady of Nohaut was a recent widow. She had brought Nohaut to her marriage as a dowry, and since her husband was a vassal of the King of Northumberland, taxes were paid to that king. The Lady's father was a liegeman of King Arthur, and since her husband was now dead, the Lady refused to continue payment to Northumberland. Nohaut was too rich a prize for the King to relinquish without a fight, but the King had no wish to go to war over it with the High King of all Britain. And so it was agreed, that champions from each side would settle the dispute.

I had sent Sir Tisant ahead to advise the Lady of our arrival. Word spread quickly, and when we entered, the town people came out into the streets and cheered. It was the first time in my young life I had been welcomed as a champion, and I confess, that I was filled with pride despite knowing that it was wrong to feel so.

The palace was surrounded by a wall intended more to define its boundaries than to be defensive. We rode through the main gate and entered a large courtyard where pages came running to help us dismount and take our horses. A squire asked me to follow him into the garden, and as I entered the Lady of Nohaut appeared.

I stopped in mid-step as if I had walked into a stone wall. Lonmarch, I swear to you, by all the gods, that the beauty in the pavilion was as a common milk maid to the Lady of Nohaut. She was astonishingly beautiful. Tall and slim with an ample bosom. She wore only a tight linen shift tied at the waist, so that every curve of her body was revealed. Her long red hair was tied back, so that her white neck showed against it. Her blue eyes, small white teeth and full lips were set in a perfect oval face. She smiled at me, and I started to shake.

My rescue came just in time. Sir Tisant came up behind me and kneeled before his Lady.

"My lady," he said, "this is Sir Lancelot. He is the knight King Arthur has sent to fight for your cause, and he is the one I told you about."

"Sir Lancelot," the Lady said in a voice that made my shaking worse, "you are most welcome. Sir Tisant will take you to your rooms where you can remove your armor, rest and make yourself comfortable. He will bring you to me, so that we may have the nighttime meal together."

I was barely able to say "Thank you, my Lady," and she smiled, turned around and walked away. I watched her every step until she disappeared.

It was necessary for Tisant to touch my arm to bring me back to my senses. As he led me into the palace, he said, "My Lady is beautiful, is she not?" I did not answer as I struggled to regain my composure.

My squires were waiting for me when I entered a room containing a large, comfortable bed, chairs and a large table, which held silver bowls filled with fruit and nuts of wide variety. Fresh washed linen trousers and a short tunic were on the bed, along with a leather belt studded with jewels and soft leather shoes. The squires had not yet seen the Lady of Nohaut and they had not seen my reaction to her, but I was short tempered with them and they knew that something was wrong. I told them to leave me alone, and when they were gone, I threw myself on the bed and stared at the ceiling.

Fighting another knight, no matter who he was, was the least of my concerns. What was I to do about the Lady of Nohaut? Her intentions toward me were no secret. My oath to Niniane, my sworn oath as an honorable knight and my secret vow to remain faithful to Guinevere weighed heavily on me, but my body surged with desire. I closed my eyes and begged the gods for guidance and help.

It was hours later when Cael shook me awake and told me that it was time for the evening meal with the Lady. I had reached a crossroad in my life, and somehow I had found the right way ahead in my sleep.

"Cael," I said, "arm me."

The young man looked at me with surprise, but something in my demeanor must have reassured him, and he did as I had asked.

When I was fully dressed for battle, I took my helmet under my arm and left the room. A page was waiting for me and he led me, with Cael behind me, through the palace until we came to the Lady's room. The page opened the door, and I immediately saw that we were in her bedchamber.

The Lady looked at me with surprise.

"Madam," I said before she could speak, "my lord King Arthur has sent me to fight for your rights, and I will defend them as soon as I may. The King has bestowed upon me this great honor in spite of my youth. His trust and my oath, as a true and pure knight, weigh heavily on me. Tonight, I will fast and pray, in my armor and with my weapons, that I will succeed in delivering you from those who are against you.

The Lady looked at me for a long while. Then she sighed and said, "Sir, I thank my lord, the King, and I thank you. I will send word that you have come, to the King of Northumberland, and that you will defend my rights, tomorrow".

I left the Lady with her page and returned to my room with Cael. Without a sound, he removed my armor as I wolfed down most of the fruit that had been my welcoming gift. Then I got into bed and slept the whole night with Cael curled up uncomfortably at the door to make sure that I would have no nocturnal visitor.

The next morning, the King of Northumberland and his followers came from where they were lodging to an open field outside of Nohaut, where the battle was to take place. The Lady of Nohaut rode out of her castle with me, my squires and her own people following. After the conditions of the battle were agreed upon and repeated, everyone, but the two champions, withdrew.

The Northumbrian knight and I rode a ways apart, then turned our horses and charged at full speed, with our lances couched. When he struck my shield with his lance, the shield splintered. But I struck his shield and drove it into his arm and chest. He was thrown over the back of his saddle and fell over his horse's tail to the ground.

The knight leaped quickly to his feet and drew his sword. I dismounted, drew my sword, and attacked. We fought furiously for some time, until the Northumbrian knight could no longer stand his ground.

I continued to attack with as much strength and speed as when we had first started, and it was clear to all who watched, that the Northumbrian knight could not survive much longer.

At last, the King of Northumberland rode between us and stopped the battle. Then he sent word to the Lady of Nohaut that he would leave her land free from any obligation.

There was great joy and celebration in Nohaut over my victory. The Lady was anxious to show her gratitude and appreciation, and invited me to stay with her as long as I wished. But I was wary of staying too long with her, and the next morning we went on our way, much to the disappointment and regret of the Lady and people of Nohaut.

Chapter 7

For almost two years after leaving Nohaut, I wandered through Britain from Cornwall to Hadrian's Wall and from the Irish Sea to the North Sea. But always I stayed away from the southeast, from Londinium to Canterbury, to avoid any encounters with someone of Arthur's court who might recognize me and report my whereabouts to the King.

I had chosen a hard life for myself. The weather was our greatest enemy. Usually it was too hot or too cold; too wet or too dry. Rain and snow in the winter and rain and heat in the summer made for a hard life without a roof over our heads, but we made our way through the country nevertheless. Sometimes the roads were impassable because of snow or flooding, and we would have to camp on high ground until conditions improved.

I could not have persevered without the wisdom, strength and loyalty of the three squires that Niniane had given me. Shelter for the night was a constant concern and Brendan's main responsibility. I could not have asked more of Brendan. More often than not, he found lodging in difficult circumstances. He was friendly and garrulous and a very handsome young man who seemed to be able to charm women of any age out of food and shelter for all of us. At every town, village and farm, he made friendly talk to glean information about where we were heading from local folk who were always superstitious and fearful of strangers. In that way, he knew how far it would be to the next castle or manor where I might sleep on a soft feather bed or to a hostel, settlement, farm, chapel or traveler's rest where a holy man would offer food and shelter.

Still, Brendan was not always successful in securing my comfort. Sometimes, I slept in a rough shed on a straw bed. Sometimes, I slept on a flea-infested cot in a hermit's cottage or on rotted straw along side farm animals. All too often, I slept outdoors, under a lean to, naked on the cool grass during the summer or wrapped tightly in everything I could find to keep warm in the winter.

Loegaire's charge was the horses, including my charger and palfrey, the three horses for the squires and two pack animals. Keeping all of the horses fed, watered, groomed, shod and healthy was hard and constant work. There never was a time when Loegaire put his comfort and wellbeing before that of the horses, and often he stood out in the rain and cold so that the beasts would be protected.

Loegaire was the oldest and the biggest of the three squires, and the other two looked to him to settle the minor disputes that occurred infrequently. I was grateful that their disagreements were never brought to me to resolve, as it would have been very difficult for me to side with one over another.

As the youngest, Cael was responsible for just about everything else, from sharpening my sword, to making a campfire and cooking a stew. Although he was born to a very noble family, he seemed to relish his place in the hierarchy of my squires and was usually cheerful in spite of the difficulties we might be in. Often, I would watch him working with a smile on his face, and I would feel a twinge of regret that I could not look upon life with such an air of optimism.

As for me, I was an errant knight, a paladin, seeking out those innocents in need of rescue or defense against outlaws and marauders. There was no King's law where

I went. If the people could not protect themselves, their only help was a wandering knight, like me, who was faithful to his vows.

My special concern was for poor women, children and old people. Everywhere we went, we found grinding poverty unlike anything I had seen on Niniane's Island. Every family on the Island had a bit of ground upon which to grow their own food or raise their own fowl, pigs or cattle. If a peasant died or was hurt or left his family, his wife and children were taken care of, and they received their share from the common stores that Niniane kept. Here in Britain, amidst the great wealth of the nobles, a widow and her children are removed from their tenancy or land, and they are left to starve if the woman cannot find work.

Under the best of circumstances, the situation of poor people is dire, and when the strong come to take from the weak, their suffering is increased many fold. But, I could serve the poor only by fighting and killing miscreants as I found them, and I could not stay in any one place. Niniane had warned me against forming attachments, and I realized that was best.

The opportunity to perform a good deed was always at hand, as the country held a great abundance of evil. Peasants, serfs, churchmen, landholders and minor noblemen usually lacked the strength or wealth to secure defenses against robbers, miscreants and murderers. Women, children and old people were always the ones who suffered most from raids. Even if they survived brutality and rape, they were worse off than they were before. I fought evil men whenever and wherever I came upon them. I attacked them with equal measures of relish and fury, and I felt no compassion for the maimed and dead men that littered my path.

Nor did I hesitate to relieve them of their horses, weapons, shields and money pouches, which often were filled to bursting. Leogaire was adept at trading weapons and horses for food and supplies we needed in our wanderings. The coins were given freely to those in need.

From the age of twelve years through adulthood, any boy or man who is landless or without tenancy is required to pay his lord a yearly tax. Landless boys are considered menials, and if they remain landless when they grow to manhood, they are condemned to the poverty of their youth. If a landless man lives by hunting or gathering, he must give most of what he has to the lord of the manor, since it is the lord's property to begin with. If a landless man works for another, such as a lord's tenant, the lord will take his payment as work or coinage, depending on how the landless earned their keep. Taxes and payments to the lord of the manor are the burdens on poor people that wear them down until they yearn for the grave and a better life with their god. Or they become embittered and angry, and they turn to the highway, where they can take from others until they are caught and hung by the neck. There was no shortage of desperate men who were forced by their poverty to turn to brigandage.

I was big and strong to begin with but, almost without noticing the changes, I continued to grow in size, strength and quickness. Living outdoors most of the time, and avoiding people and animals in confined spaces, seemed to contribute to my natural good health so that I was rarely sick. But, my greatest advantage in war was my breath. I had trained myself to remain calm and breathe slowly and deeply during battle. While my opponent was panting like a dog, I breathed normally. It was inevitable that after beating on each other, with all of our strength, for some time, that the other fellow would be gasping, with his tongue hanging out, while I still had the energy to overwhelm him. With every encounter, I became wiser and more skillful. I learned something from every combatant.

My practice of fighting all comers who used every imaginable weapon gave me experience that I could never have gained jousting against other knights in tournaments or formal fights where we were both expected to obey the rules.

Fighting a trained knight was usually a straightforward affair. I knew beforehand what he would do with a lance or a spear. There was not much in the way of tactics, except for aiming at my shield or helmet. Battle with a short sword, while mounted, was a matter of battering each other's shields or getting a fortunate swipe at a thigh or helmet. Fighting on foot with two-handed swords, clubs or maces was by far the most dangerous.

I had to be careful of the ground around me and alert to any obstacles. Falling backward on a rock or tree root could be disastrous. Shadows and light continuously changed as my position changed. Finally, if the other knight had experience fighting ruffians, there would be feints and tricks that were not part of the classical training.

Ultimately, fighting another knight meant physically beating him until he was too weak, from loss of blood or otherwise, to defend himself, and he either yielded or took a blow that ended it all.

Dealing with untrained, rough and tumble fighters was altogether different. Their weapons and styles were always personalized. They were generally unencumbered by armor or any sense of chivalry or fairness. Retreat or escape held no dishonor for them. Mercy towards a fallen opponent was foreign to their code. Ambush, night attack, attacking from behind: any means of taking down a knight for his horse, armor or anything else of value was acceptable.

The one constant in my life was fighting. I fought the highborn and the lowborn. I killed thieves, rapists and murderers. I killed strong and well-armored fighting men who traveled alone and took what they wanted when they saw it. I slaughtered bands of men who used their strength of numbers to intimidate villages and settlements and take food, animals and women as they wished.

My favorite target for retribution were fallen knights; those who had abandoned their vows and lived off the land, not like me, but by stealing for their own gain and murdering and raping for their own pleasure. Those men had trained as knights, received the accolade and had sworn to live by a code of honor. They had the strength and prowess to exceed all others in robbing, murdering, rape, kidnapping and extortion.

Only slightly less of a favorite were lowborn men who wore a murdered knight's armor and used that title in order to exert rights and authority over others for their own gain. These false knights were everywhere. They roamed the countryside and took what they wanted. Sometimes, they raided on their own, but more often, they came with a band of cutthroats and pirates. They were not content to steal grain and animals, women and children and everything of value. They wanted to be feared, and so they burned what they left.

Fighting from spring to autumn was easy, but fighting in winter was a special challenge. Using a lance or spear in the rain or snow was impossible, since the horses could not move at anything like full speed. Battles were on foot, and I made use of every weapon I had, depending on the enemy. Most of the time, I used the short sword, but I also used the axe, mace and the two-handed long sword. Sometimes it came down to a poniard, especially when a fight degenerated to wrestling on the ground. A heavy club was the weapon of choice in a close melee.

I learned early on to use discretion, slyness and outright trickery. Often I used my squires as a decoy or diversion, while I flanked my opponents and caught them by surprise. Sometimes I allowed Loegaire to fight in my armor, since he was close to knighthood and a practiced killer in his own right (as were the other squires).

For some reason I cannot forget the first man I killed. He was a peasant who had turned outlaw and he and his small band of six other cohorts must have been desperate indeed to attack an armed and mounted knight and three armed and mounted squires. One man leaped out of cover to confront me with an axe. The others attacked at the rear with a motley collection of weapons including swords and spiked clubs.

Without any signal from me, Fer de Blanc surged forward and knocked the man off balance. My sword was out in an instant and I swung it down from my left shoulder. It bit into the man's right shoulder and sliced diagonally into his chest. I had time only to see his eyes widen as I kicked him free of my sword and turned to assist my squires.

The rest of the band had seen the blow I had given their leader and they ran for cover, most of them bleeding from wounds given by my young warriors.

I could not overcome my curiosity and rode back to look at the dead man. He was sprawled on the ground with his head thrown back. His eyes were open as was his mouth as if his jaw was unhinged. His jerkin was soaked with blood and black blood pooled under him.

I felt my stomach tighten and sour bile started to rise in my throat. I wanted to puke but I knew my squires were watching me. I swallowed my disgust and kicked Fer de Blanc into a trot away from the site of my first kill.

There came a time, soon enough, when the sight of fresh blood no longer bothered me unless it was my own (which happened infrequently).

I had no pity for the violence I delivered to the low miscreants, who lived off the hard work of innocents. Unfortunately, I also learned that those whom I considered innocent were not always so. It seemed like everyone took from someone else according to his strength and opportunity. My pity and service were often misdirected. A victim of theft could just as well be a thief himself. A victim of rape might be a murderess of her own newborn infant. Holy men might be voracious fornicators or abusers of children. The lives of the poor and landless were deemed worthless by their betters and their own selves. Under such miserable circumstances, true Christian charity and love was a rare and dim light in the darkness.

Although I tried to avoid it, there were times when I encountered one of Arthur's knights. These were opportunities to test my prowess against the very best of knighthood. At each of these contests, I left my opponent laying disarmed on the field, nursing some kind of injury. Because of these outcomes, stories started to spread at Arthur's court about a White

Knight, who seemed invincible, but would not share his name with his vanquished foe.

The itinerant life was a terrible strain on the horses, my squires and me. Even worse was the growing doubt that anything good I did made any real or lasting difference in the world. I was sure that after I had done something useful somewhere, and moved on, everything went back to the way it was before.

Chapter 8

There was nothing more to prove to myself or anyone else about my courage and my prowess, and I started to think more about my future. If I returned to Arthur's court, I would be nothing more than his warrior. I would have to fight his wars, collect his tributes and defend him against challengers. It seemed a bleak future, but there was not much else I could do. Still, it was time to stop this wandering for a while, and I was anxious to see my cousins, as well as Gawain and Yvain, and especially "my friend," the Queen.

We had traveled the countryside for days, on the roads toward Londinium, without a single adventure to speak of when good fortune finally came my way at a narrow bridge crossing a modest stream.

By the time I reached the bridge, a mounted knight was already on the other side of the stream waiting for me. He was a big man, well horsed and armored. The squires waiting behind him were richly horsed and dressed as well. He was not wearing his helmet and his handsome face bore a merry smile indicating that his delight in encountering me was as great as my own. There was no doubt in my mind that I was facing a knight of considerable honor and prowess and that our meeting would be exciting and worthwhile.

"Will you let me pass, sir?" he shouted, "I was here before you."

"You may indeed cross first with my good wishes," I answered, "if you will first agree to do me the honor of jousting with me."

"Well said," he replied, "that I will gladly do."

The knight and his squires crossed the bridge and rode a short way to one end of a clearing where we would have room to run our horses at each other. He dismounted his palfrey and one of his squires helped him with his helmet. Then, after he was remounted on a very fine chestnut charger, another page handed him a shield and a lance with not a single mark on either one.

I, too, was fully armed except for my helmet, When I was remounted on Le Fer de Blanc and had my helmet in place, I rode to the opposite side of the clearing and couched my lance. I nodded that I was ready. The other knight drove his heels into his mount and we charged each other at full speed.

My chest was pounding as if I would burst. My thighs and legs gripped as tight as they could. Every bit of me became tensed, and I could see nothing but my adversary coming at me so slowly that I thought it would take forever before I could reach him.

Of course, it was over in an instant. My lance struck him to the left of the center of his shield and, while his shield held, my lance splintered into useless kindling. His lance struck the center of my shield, broke it in half and drove through it. His lance struck my left epauliere. Fortunately, I had turned slightly in my saddle, and it was only a glancing blow that did no harm. I rode back and Brandon handed me another lance and shield. Once again, we charged and, again, my lance and shield shattered, while the effect on my foe was negligible. I was furious at my failure as I rode back once more for another lance and shield. This time I swore to myself the result would be different. Indeed it was. This third time, I was lifted out of my saddle, went flying through the air, and landed on the ground on my ass.

The knight dismounted, drew his sword and came towards me. This was an entirely new experience for me, and I laughed thinking to myself that my days as a hero were over and I was about to die. But, as the knight approached, he held out his open mailed hand and helped me regain my feet. When he saw that I was steady and unharmed in every way but pride, he put himself en Garde and waited for me to draw my sword.

When I, too, was en Garde, he swung at me with all of his strength. I caught his blade edge on mine, and my sword broke in half. He immediately lowered his weapon and invited me to obtain another sword. Brandon came running up with one I had never used before, and we began to swing and hack at each other with great enthusiasm. I soon realized that his skill and strength with a sword did not match his prowess with a lance. I avoided catching his sword with mine, edge-to-edge, and beat on his shield with ever increasing ferocity. We fought for almost an hour, with him attacking while I kept circling, in order to avoid his sword and hitting him whenever I could. Finally, he fell to his knees gasping for breath and held up his open right hand.

"I am done. I yield to you, sir," he said as he stretched out on the grass. "You may do with me as you wish."

I sat down on the grass next to him, flung my sword to the side and motioned to Brendan to come and remove my helmet. "Sir," I answered, " I thank you for this delightful exercise and I thank you for your gracious and knightly courtesy. I have no further intentions for you. You have no obligation to me, and you are a free man. But I do have four requests of you which you may freely refuse without dishonor."

"Ask what you will, sir, and if I can comply, you will be satisfied."

"First, I wish to know your name."

"That desire is easily satisfied," he said as his squire removed his helmet. "My name is Sir Taygar, and I am the lord of Bristol Castle and all of the lands hereabout.

"What are the other three desires?"

"I wish to have your lance, shield and sword."

"Ah, sir knight, I would rather you take everything I have other than those three, but they are yours by right. They will be sorely missed, for they have given me great service. Nevertheless, I would have them give you the great service they have given me, for there are no stronger weapons anywhere, and they may have powers of their own since I have unhorsed many knights whose prowess is greater than mine."

"Who are the makers of these weapons, and how did you come by them?"

"I know nothing of their provenance. I found them beside a knight who was dying. He was alone, without either a squire or page to attend him and witness his death. He was of middle age and without a mortal wound anywhere on his body. So I have no knowledge of where they came from or of what they are made."

Sir Taygar was a pleasant companion who told interesting stories of his adventures, which I only half listened to, while I examined my new weapons carefully. My shields were small and round, made of wood, with an iron band around the outside edge and an iron boss in the center. The knight's shield was rounded at the top and tapered toward the bottom, thus giving far greater protection to the user. It was not made of wood, but of several layers of the hide of an animal that seemed unknown to me. The hides had been sewn together, and treated somehow, so that the layers acted as one. The whole appeared as if no sword or arrow could penetrate it and no lance could split it. Inside, in the center, was a pair of leather grips, which I could hold in my hand or strap to my forearm. It was decorated with painted inscriptions, which I could not decipher, and the outside edge was banded with gold.

The knight's sword was also a great surprise to me. My sword had only one sharpened edge and a rounded tip. It was a weapon to be used much like a hammer; beating on a shield until there was an opening, and then slicing into an arm or a leg and finally, lopping off a head. His sword was narrower than mine, but both edges were sharpened and it had a sharp tapered point, which could be used for thrusting with either hand or with both hands. Unlike my sword, which would not bend, Sir Taygar's sword formed a slight arc when I braced the tip and leaned against it. The blade itself had patterns on it, which I had never seen before.

The lance was made of the hardest wood I had ever encountered. It was only with great effort that I was able to put a small notch in it with my knife. Unlike my lances, which had iron tips, Sir Taygars lance tip appeared to be made of the same metal as the sword.

We spent the rest of the day and that night resting near the bridge by the stream. We slept in a very fine pavilion that the knight's pages took down from packhorses and erected under a magnificent oak. The next morning, after eating, we parted ways, with me the richer for possession of a truly remarkable lance, sword and shield.

As we followed a narrow path through a forest, I thought about my life, and I realized that I was not like most other knights. Many of the knights in Arthur's court were not of noble families. They were fighters who traded their services in war for the parcels of land they held in fief from the King. They, in turn, depended on rents from tenants and taxes from peasants who work their land. Other knights in Arthur's court were the sons, especially the younger sons, of noble families. They were the knights who had received the accolade, and had sworn themselves to a life of honor and duty. Still, unless they held land from their families, they had to rely on Arthur's largesse.

Gawain and his brothers, and the other sons of rich and powerful kings, spent most of their time around Arthur. Their daily lives were taken up with hunting, practice with weapons, tournaments, jousting, feasting and games. They had seneschals and other underlings who took care of their lands, manors and castles.

The knights who depended on their lands to sustain them, had to spend much of their time at their farms and manors. They dealt with rents and taxes, decisions on which crops to plant and when to buy and sell livestock. They resolved disputes and enforced the laws. They trained and exercised their tenants in archery and other weapons so they would be ready for war when the King called them. These knights also defended their fiefs against thieves, murderers and those who would take their land from them.

I owed fealty to King Arthur, but I did not hold land from him. I had no obligation to fight his wars, although I would do so out of loyalty and gratitude. I did not sit around a manor house worrying about crops and cattle. I earned my keep by the sweat of my brow. I served kings and peasants, and I was rewarded with friendship and generosity. I went and came as I pleased. I fought for someone only for love, duty or honor, not to pay a debt.

I was, and I still am, a free man.

Chapter 9

Just before mid-day, we came out onto a broad road which forked in two directions. As I pondered which direction to take, a veiled lady appeared riding a fine palfrey and followed by two finely dressed squires. I saluted her and she stopped.

"Lady," I said, "can you tell me what lies down each fork of this road?"

"My lord," she answered, "to the left lies King Arthur's encampment. There are many knights with him, and they are searching for the knight who fought on behalf of the Lady of Nohaut. Word has spread of that knight's great prowess, and the King and his court wish to honor him.

"To the right lies a castle. If you try to enter there, it will surely mean your death."

"Lady, can you tell me anything about this castle?"

"My lord, the castle is on a hill and is protected by two walls, one inside the other. It is known, far and wide, as Dolorous Garde. The lord of that castle is a baron of great evil intent and practice. The people of his country are held as slaves. There is no freedom or justice for the common folk. The baron has forty knights who fear him and obey him in all things, whether honorable or not. They rob and kill innocent travelers and traders who dare to pass through his country. They collect taxes from even the poorest. They force the people to labor in the baron's fields and manors, when their own fields need harvest. If a tenant protests, he loses his land and his freedom. All the people of this land live in fear of the baron and his knights, but they are unable to flee or find succor from their suffering."

"Why does King Arthur or some brave knight not put an end to this sad place?"

"Sir knight, no king dares to lay siege to the castle for fear that the baron will slay the knights that he keeps prisoner in his dungeons for ransom. Many knights have tried to gain entrance to the castle through the first gate, but every one of them has been slain or taken prisoner."

"What must I do to enter that castle?"

"Sir, knight, you must ride up the hill to the first gate and strike it loudly with your lance. The gatekeeper will appear and ask you what you want. Answer that you will do battle, with whoever you must, in order to enter the castle. The gate keeper will instruct you to ride back down to the plain at the base of the castle and wait for a knight to come down and joust with you.

"Sir knight, there are two walls around the castle with a gate in each wall. At each gate, any knight who wishes to enter must fight and defeat ten knights, one at a time. But, as soon as one knight is tired and does not wish to fight any longer, the next knight takes his place. No single knight can defeat them all, unless he is able to defeat one after the other. They will each come down to fight you, until you can fight no more, and then one of them will kill you or take you prisoner."

"What will happen," I asked, "if I defeat all of those knights?"

"I do not know, my lord, since that has never happened and I fear it never will."

As I listened to what the lady said, I began to fix in my own thoughts what lay before me. Dolorous Garde was my destiny. I would either win this trial and gain everlasting honor, or I would die with honor, but I would not allow myself to be taken alive to rot in a dungeon.

I knew that I had great strength, and I no longer doubted my courage. The baron's knights would face an opponent unlike any they had met before. I would maim or kill every one of them, as quickly as possible, and then do whatever I must to enter the castle and drive out the evil and fearsome tyrant and all of his minions.

I would free the people of this country, and there would be joy in place of sorrow, loyalty in place of hate. I would enforce justice and mercy. I would not tax those too poor to pay. My cousins and I and our liegemen would protect this country so that freemen, villeins, peasants and serfs would live and work in peace and safety.

I would call the castle Joyous Garde, and I would be the lord of the castle and all of the land appertaining to it. Without land, I would be no more than a bond-servant, no more than my name implies. As I was, I was no better than other knights who were not noblemen and had to fight with the sword and lance to earn their keep. As the master of Joyous Garde, I would no longer be landless and beholden to the generosity of others, including Niniane. That would be my home and my fortress, and I would be a lord for the first time in my life.

As these thoughts and plans flowed through me, I had ridden slowly up the switchbacks to the top of the hill and stopped at the large wooden gate. I shook myself out of my daydreaming and beat on the gate with the butt of my lance.

An old man, who must have been watching me approach, leaned over the rampart to the side of the gate.

"What may I do for you, sir knight?"

"Let me in," I answered.

"That I may not do though it would give me great joy to do so. Go down from here, sir, and never return. If you persist in this adventure, you will surely die, and it would be a great shame for so young and handsome a knight, as yourself, to perish from this world."

"Thank you for your kind warning, sir but I will do what I must to enter this castle."

"Alas, then, sir knight. Go down from here and wait on the plain below. A knight from this castle will go down and joust with you. There are ten knights behind the gate. When you hear a horn blow, another one of those knights will go down to do battle. You must defeat all ten knights, and prevent them from returning to the castle, if you wish to enter this gate."

I rode back down the hill to where my squires and the veiled lady were waiting.

"Be vigilant," I said. "You may not interfere with anything that happens to me, but you must bring me a shield, sword or lance if I need one. Do not come to my aid if I am wounded or unhorsed. I will either be victorious or I will die on this field."

Then, with my helmet in place and my lance couched, I rode towards a clear area and turned, so that my back was toward the sun.

I did not have to wait long. Someone blew a horn in the castle and the gate opened. A fully armed knight rode through the gate and down the hill. As soon as he reached the plain, he couched his lance, spurred his charger and galloped full-tilt toward me.

We came together, with all the speed our horses could muster, and collided. I remained well seated as his lance shattered on my shield. My lance passed under his shield, pierced his chain mail and went through his side. As we passed, he hung onto his saddle and screamed in pain as my lance tore through his body and came free. He wavered from side to side as he struggled to remain in the saddle. With a great effort, he righted himself and turned his horse's head toward the castle.

The horn had blown again, and another knight was urging his horse down the hill. I did not have much time. I drove my lance into the ground, drew my sword and kicked Fer de Blanc into a gallop. As soon as I drew alongside the wounded knight, I swung my sword and separated his head from his body.

I turned Fer de Blanc and galloped back to where my lance stood, stuck in the ground, waiting for me.

The second knight charged at me and I tossed him over the back of his horse when we collided. I could not bring myself to kill him with my lance as he struggled to his feet in a daze. But the horn sounded again, and the third knight was on the way to rescue his companion. I dismounted, drew my sword and ran over to the knight who had gotten to his knees.

"Sir knight," I yelled, "will you fight or will you yield?"

"I yield, my lord. Let me go to your squires and I will be your faithful liegeman for the rest of my life."

"Go then. Leave this field."

As the knight rose unsteadily to his feet and turned away, I felt the thundering hoof beats of the third knight approaching. It was too late for me to remount. I let the knight come at me directly at full speed but at the last instant, I leaped away from his lance and caught the horse's bridle. With all my strength, I pulled the horse off balance and both he and his rider crashed to the ground. The knight kicked himself free of the struggling mount and leaped to his feet with his sword in his hand and his shield before him.

I ran up to the knight and swung my sword with all my might an instant before I crashed into him. He stumbled backwards, and I smashed my shield into his body. Already off balance, he fell backwards to the ground.

"Yield or die," I growled as I kicked his shield away and pointed my sword at his chest.

"I will yield to you in Hades," he cursed.

I drove my sword into him. He squirmed briefly and died.

The fourth knight must not have been too anxious to meet his fate, for I had ample time to retrieve my lance and remount. So far, I was unhurt and though I was breathing heavily, it was more from excitement than fatigue. What was more important was that Fer de Blanc seemed fresh, and my lance and shield, though sprayed red with blood, were still undamaged.

Confidence flowed through me. If this was the worst I would have to deal with, the outcome was assured. After I dispatched the fourth knight, the horn blew six more times. In the end, of the ten knights sent against me, three were unhorsed and severely injured (perhaps mortally), four were killed on the spot with the lance or sword and three yielded. With the defeat of the last knight, a portal in the castle wall opened, and squires, pages, surgeons and litter bearers came streaming out, rushing to aid their masters.

Then the horn blew no more and there were no more knights to fight. Under my armor, my body was soaking wet and sweat was burning my eyes. In spite of that, my mouth was so dry that I could barely swallow. I tore off my helmet, threw it to the ground and dried my eyes with a scarf tied around my neck. I breathed in the fresh air and felt wild and restless.

Fer de Blanc's flanks were heaving and flecked with foam, but he was as filled with nervous energy as I was, and I let him prance with impatience and paw the ground.

I looked around at the bloody field. I had defeated ten knights. I was invincible. I was a messenger of death. Nothing could stop me. I rose up in my stirrups and pumped my sword and left fist in the air. The blood lust was upon me.

"I am Lancelot," I screamed at the top of my lungs. "I am Lancelot," I screamed again and kicked Fer de Blanc into a gallop back up the hill. I sped through the first gate and came to a sliding halt at the second.

"Open the gate," I roared.

The old man who had spoken to me earlier leaned over the parapet.

"Sir knight, as you are a noble and honorable knight, my master begs that you return tomorrow morning when you will surely be welcomed."

"No," I yelled, "tell your master that if he and his knights will not fight me now, then they are all craven cowards."

"Sir knight,' the old man replied, "there will be no further battle today." And with that, he disappeared.

So once more, I rode down the hill. By then, I had calmed myself and regained my senses. Without a helmet and lance, and with a tired horse, I would not have fared too well. My squires and the mysterious lady with the veil were waiting for me. She held her open palm toward me as I approached.

"Sir knight," she said, "you have done well. Do not regret that you cannot continue this battle today. If you come with me now, I will take you to a villa nearby, where you can rest and refresh yourself and prepare for tomorrow. I assure you that your welcome tomorrow morning at the castle will not be friendly or gentle. You will need all of your courage and prowess to continue, if that is what you want to do."

"I assure you, lady, that I will see this adventure through to its end even if you assure me of my death. But for now, I will follow where you lead. My squires need rest as well, since their great concern on my behalf has exhausted them."

We followed the damsel through the town to the north side of the castle, where she had very fine lodgings. Pages and squires appeared as if by magic, and we were helped to dismount and remove our armor. My squires and all of the horses were led away to be fed and cared for while the damsel took me by the arm and took me through the villa and into a brightly lit chamber. The lady left me while servants bathed me and dressed me in fresh linen clothes and brought in a great variety of food and wine.

In a short while, she returned. Now she was very richly dressed and her face was uncovered.

When I turned and looked at the damsel's face I recognized her immediately and embraced her with great love and devotion.

"My dear Saraide," I said, "I can not say how pleased and happy I am to see you here now and know that you have been watching over me. But first, tell me, how is the health of my Lady Niniane?"

"She is very well and bids me remind you of her love and good wishes for you. She has sent me to you to tell you that tomorrow you will learn your true name, and the name of your father and mother. But first, you must conquer this castle, make it your own and put an end to the evil that it spreads. Tomorrow, before night falls, you must defeat ten more knights who are waiting for you at the second gate and who will defend it to the death."

Like a child, I thought that finally I would know who I really was and all of my questions would be answered. My excitement at this wonderful news made me feel as if I could conquer every knight in Britain. I could not restrain myself from asking questions but Saraide would not answer them. For a while, Saraide and I sat and talked of many other things as we ate our evening meal. Then I went to a richly furnished bed and slept deeply and peacefully.

In the morning, Saraide helped me into my armor and rode with me and our squires and knights towards the castle hill. When we reached the meadow at the foot of castle, we saw that three pavilions had been erected for the knights that I had fought the previous day who were injured but still alive. Immediately upon seeing us, a squire ran up to me and bowed deeply.

"My lord," he said, "my lord, Sir Gregoire, to whom you showed mercy and who has sworn loyalty and fealty to you, begs that you come to him before you face today's battle."

I nodded my head in agreement and followed the squire to his lord's pavilion. Sir Gregoire was resting on a cot. His bandages were red with his blood, but he seemed calm, and there was no paleness in his face. When he spoke, his voice was strong and that gave me hope that he would survive his injuries.

As soon as I approached, he began to speak.

"My lord, the deeds you performed yesterday are without equal, and there is no doubt that you are without peer. But, today's challenge is much greater than what you have already faced and overcome. When you go up the hill, you will find that the first gate is open to you but the second gate is closed. Before you reach the second gate, a horn will sound and the second gate will open. However, this time you will not fight one knight at a time. There will be ten knights waiting behind the gate, and when it opens, they will attack you all at once.

"My lord, if you are without fear, you can still overcome those knights. The place they will wait for you is a long, narrow alley. There is no room to wield a lance or sword. If you trust my advice, you will drop your lance as soon as the gate opens and charge into that alley with an axe or club. The knights will not have room to wield their swords or lances either, and you will take them by surprise."

"Sir Gregoire," I said, "I trust you, and I will do just as you advise. If I survive this challenge, I will release you from your oaths and you will be a free man."

"Sir knight, if you survive, I will have no wish in life other than to be your man and serve you as well as I might."

I shook Gregoire's hand, left the pavilion and mounted the well-rested Fer de Blanc.

As I thought about what was about to happen, I became more and more angry, and my anger grew into a rage. These were the basest of knights. These were knights without honor and not fit to bear the title of knight. They deserved to die, not by the lance or sword, but by the most ignoble of weapons; the club.

I was fully armed, except for my helmet. Cael placed it on my head and helped me mount Fer de Blanc. Brendan handed me my lance and I started toward the castle at a trot. I thought about what was ahead of me. Clearly, this was a challenge that Niniane had known about, if not planned, all along, since Saraide was not waiting for me at the crossroads by happenstance. Did Niniane have me in the palm of her hand? Had she arranged for me to meet the test of the first gate? Was I fated to win the second gate through Niniane's magic or was my fate in my own hands.

I shook my head to clear it of the thoughts and questions that had no answers and tried to think about the upcoming fight.

I rode up the hill to the castle and saw the first gate wide open in front of me. Unlike the last time I had been there, I was eager, yet calm, and thinking about what I was about to do.

As soon as I heard the horn blow and the creak of the second gate's hinges, I dropped my lance, grabbed the heavy club bristling with iron spikes that hung from my saddle, and spurred my horse into a furious charge.

A horse, even a trained warhorse, will refuse to charge headlong into a solid wall of defenders, whether they are mounted or on foot. But Fer de Blanc is different. He will break into a massed wall of foot soldiers or mounted knights without hesitation and, therein, was my great advantage.

As soon as the gate was opened wide enough, I charged into the mass of mounted knights who were waiting for me. They had expected me to attack with my lance, and so the knights in front of the pack had their own lances couched. They had no time to charge forward, as Fer de Blanc was upon them in an instant. I brushed the lance of the first knight aside and crushed his helmet with my club. He screamed and started to fall from his saddle. All at once, there was mayhem, with some knights trying to attack me while others were trying to escape. I continued to charge through the confusion with a single purpose. Sir Gregoire was right, this was no place for a lance or a sword. Every time I swung the club, the results were devastating. The knights in front of me blocked those in back, and they kept trying to retreat under my onslaught. I kept driving them backwards into the small space in the alley, so that no other knights in the castle could enter and come to their rescue. The screaming and crazed horses added to the frenzy as Fer de Blanc increased their misery with bites and kicks.

It was over in just minutes. Dead and injured knights lay one on top of the other. Injured horses stood stunned with hanging heads. Not one knight had been able to avoid me. I sat quietly on my horse, breathing heavily, as I looked over the carnage. Blood was everywhere, Fer de Blanc and I were covered with it.

I smiled with self satisfaction. Niniane had led me here, but this was all my own doing, not hers. She may lead me here or there, but, in the end, it is my arms and my will that face and defeat death.

I backed Fer de Lance out of that tiny battlefield and rode slowly down the hill. People from the town were already running toward the meadow jumping, cheering, and making a great noise. I kept on in amazement, as the crowd turned then swarmed around me, yelling and screaming with joy and hailing me as the conqueror and deliverer of Dolorous Garde.

These were my people now. These were the shopkeepers and tradesmen, masons, farriers, stockmen, farmers, peasants, villeins, serfs and freemen who had been miserably oppressed and now looked hopefully to me to improve their lives. I saw my squires trying to reach me, but they could not get through the happy crowd. I pulled my helmet off and dropped it to the ground. I pulled off my chain mail gloves and dropped them, as well. Then I reached down and touched every hand that was raised to me. I watched the smiling faces of the people, and I felt my own smile and a joy I had never felt before.

When I finally reached the pavilions, the crowd had been dispersed by Loegaire, who told the people that I had to rest and that I would come and talk to them as soon as I could. Sir Gregoire was waiting for me, standing between two squires who held him up.

I went immediately to the wounded knight.

"Sir Gregoire," I said, "I have much to thank you for."

"My, lord," he answered with a wide grin on his face, "it is I who have you to thank. You are the answer to my prayers, for I am sure that you will do what is just and honorable in all things. That is why I have done what I could to help you, and that is why I ask a boon of you."

"Ask what you will. If it is in my power, I will grant what you ask."

"My lord, there is a prison near here called Dolorous Prison. The Baron has many knights locked away for ransom. One of those knights is my brother, Sir Vannes. The only way that I could pay my brother's ransom was to fight for the Baron. I beg you to free those knights."

As Gregoire spoke, I felt the rage build in me again. I would not hesitate. I would free those knights immediately and kill that Baron, if it took forever to find him. But before I could give orders to my squires, Saraide came up to me and took my arm.

"Dear knight, before you go, you must come with me."

Saraide led me through another portal in the castle wall to a small cemetery partially hidden between the two outer castle walls. On the tombs were the names of many good knights from King Arthur's court and from foreign lands as well. In the furthest, darkest corner of the cemetery, she pointed out a thick iron plate, the length and width of a grave, covered with dirt, old leaves and broken branches.

"Dear knight," said Saraide, "you must raise that plate for then you will learn who you are and where your final resting place will be."

I brushed aside the debris and took hold of one end of the plate, which was a great weight, and raised it over my head. Under it, I saw writing, which said,

"Here lies Lancelot of the Lake, who was born Galahad, the son of King Ban and Queen Helen of Benoic in Brittany."

I lowered the plate slowly. I felt like everything was whirling before my eyes. This is what I had yearned to know all of my life, yet it was difficult for me to comprehend. Questions flooded my mind. What had happened to my father and mother? Did I have any brothers or sisters? Why was I raised by Niniane? Would this truly be my final resting place?

I took a deep breath and regained my composure. For now, what was important was that, for the first time in my life, I truly knew who I was and from where I had come. I was the son of a great and noble knight and king and I would never need to lower my eyes before any King or Queen in the world. I would ask for answers later.

As Saraide and I left the cemetery, people of the castle, who had been searching for me, surrounded us, and I tried to put my confused thoughts out of my head. I could not bring myself to deny the desire of my people to welcome me, and I allowed them to take me to a beautiful hall where they disarmed me and treated me with great honor and respect, as their new lord and master. All through these happy events, I churned at the thought of the imprisoned knights, but first, I had to secure the castle and land that was now mine.

There were a great many people of all stations in life in the hall, and I knew that what I said here would be spread throughout my domain. I stood on a chair and raised my hand for quiet.

"I am called Lancelot of the Lake. I am a knight of King Arthur's court, and I received the accolade from him. I pledge to you that evil and lawless men will no longer rule this country. As I am a true and honorable knight, I give you my oath that justice and fairness will prevail for all. No longer will this castle be Dolorous Garde. It is to be known from now on as Joyous Garde, and I claim this castle and the town and lands hereabout for myself and for no other. Sir Gregoire shall be my seneschal and I shall be your guardian and guarantor of peace and prosperity."

It was by far the longest speech I had ever made and by the cheering, the most well received.

With that duty carried out, I turned my thoughts to the knights still imprisoned and the escaped knights of Dolorous Garde. The next morning, I left my castle at first light with Brendan, Loegaire and Cael and one of Gregoire's pages to guide us.

As soon as we left Joyous Garde, Sir Gregoire dispatched a squire to Arthur's court with instructions to tell the King everything that had happened. The lad's older brother was one of Arthur's knights and he brought the squire before the King as soon as he heard the news himself. Gawain was with the King and he later related to me all that was said and decided.

"My lord, Arthur," said the squire, "a single knight has conquered Dolorous Garde. He overcame twenty knights by his own strength and courage and forced his entry through the two gates whose defenses were scant barriers to his prowess."

The king could not believe what he had just heard. There were shouts of "Impossible," and "You lie," from the crowd of courtiers around the King.

"I tell the truth, my Lord," said the youth, "I saw him go into the castle and defeat the knights at both gates with my own eyes. What would I gain by lying?"

"What arms did that knight carry?" asked the King.

"He had a large shield banded in gold, a great lance that did not break and a great white destrier, the likes of which I have never seen or heard of."

Gawain immediately surmised the truth. He spoke up and suggested, to the King, that the conqueror of Dolorous Garde was the young squire who had been brought to him by the lady in white. He reminded Arthur that he had made the young man a knight not so long ago, and had sent him to defend the rights of the Lady of Nohaut. Then he told the King that he wished to go and see for himself if indeed it was that young knight who had overthrown Dolorous Castle.

The King agreed, but ordered that Sir Yvain and eight other knights accompany Gawain on the search. So, the knights and their squires left Westminster and rode for ten days, until they reached the castle that had been called Dolorous Garde. As they approached the castle and rode up the hill, they found that the gates were wide open. When they entered and made known that they were King Arthur's knights, they were welcomed with great warmth and hospitality and taken to see Sir Gregoire, who was delighted to welcome them and to relate everything that had occurred.

As the curious and excited people gathered around, Gawain asked what knight had freed the castle and where he was. "Sir knight," Gregoire answered, "his name is Sir Lancelot of the Lake. He has gone to free many knights who have been imprisoned, and to find and destroy the former lord of this castle. He has charged me to beg you to remain here until he returns."

After leaving Joyous Garde we rode all day until we came through a small wood and out to a meadow beneath a hill. There stood the small castle known as Dolorous Prison.

"Young man," I said to Gregoire's page "do you know of any way that I can enter that castle?"

"No, my lord," he answered, "but every night, the knights, who defend the prison, ride out to do mischief in the countryside and rob or kill innocent travelers."

I said no more but rode back into the wood, where we could wait and watch the castle gate unseen. That night, when the moon began to rise, twenty knights rode out of the castle gate in troop formation.

I had learned my lessons well. My plan of attack was simple but direct. I chose a place where the path narrowed, so that the oncoming knights would be forced to ride two abreast. What would make matters worse for them was that the path had a high crown with sides that sloped steeply away into underbrush. As the leading knights appeared, I drove Fer de Blanc into a gallop and in seconds, I collided with the head of the column at full speed.

The knights were taken by surprise. As Fer de Blanc shouldered his way between the stunned riders, their horses were forced to sidestep and they struggled to maintain their footing. The knights were distracted by their efforts to maintain their saddles, as I hurtled between them, swinging left and right at their heads and arms with my heavy club.

By the time I had completed my bloody passage through the column, more than half of the stunned and battered knights were on the ground. I reined in Fer de Blanc and reversed his course, riding back towards the remaining mounted knights. The path was too narrow and littered with bodies for the knights to turn their panicked horses, so that now their backs were toward me. I barreled through them once more, bashing heads and breaking arms.

I turned again to charge through the column once again, but I saw that I had done all that I could. Unfortunately, four of the knights had managed to escape.

I dismounted and surveyed the carnage, searching the path, littered with broken bodies, until I heard a knight moaning. I approached the knight, knelt by his side and removed his helmet. Then I raised my sword as if to separate his head from his neck and said, "Sir, I will kill you instantly for your crimes, or I will show you mercy and spare your life if you yield to me and swear to obey my wishes."

"My lord," the knight answered, " I agree to yield, and I will do as you wish in return for my life."

"Go up to the prison," I said, "and free all of the knights who are held there. Tell Sir Vannes that his brother, Sir Gregoire, is now seneschal of the castle that was called Dolorous Garde. Beg him and all of the other knights to go to that castle and wait there until the knight who has set them free returns. Ask him also to make welcome any knight of King Arthur's court."

The wounded knight was only too happy to agree. He mounted a horse that Brendan brought to him, and rode off slowly to the prison, as the rest of us continued in the direction taken by the knights who had escaped me.

We searched through the night and the next day. The following morning, as we rode out of a forest and onto an open plain, we saw four fully armed knights resting on the ground. As soon as the knights caught sight of us, they began to cry, "To horse! To horse! Flee! Flee!" and they leaped on their horses and spurred them furiously across the plain, hoping to escape into the woods.

One of the knights was more richly dressed and armed than the others, and I knew that it was he who was the Baron of Dolorous Garde. I raced after him. His horse could not match the speed or endurance of mine, and as I caught up to him, I struck him on the helmet with my sword and stunned him, so that he had to hold on to his horse's neck with both arms to keep from falling. Then, I grasped him by the plume on his helmet and pulled him out of the saddle. He fell to the ground in a faint. I dismounted, walked up to him and pulled off his helmet. Without a word, I struck off his head.

With the death of the Baron of Dolorous Garde, the castle, town and lands were truly mine.

When we returned to Joyous Garde we found Gawain and all of the other knights enjoying the comforts of the castle and the hospitality of my people. What followed were feasts, celebrations and games for all to enjoy and the distribution of land and monies that rightfully belonged to the highborn and lowborn of Joyous Garde.

After many happy days Gawain sent word to the King to assure him that the White Knight had indeed taken Dolorous Garde and that all of his knights, being held for ransom had been freed. When the duration of our celebrations and good fellowship exceeded Arthur's patience he sent word back to Joyous Garde sternly requesting that Gawain, Yvain, the White Knight and all the other knights come to him at Londinium. I could not disobey that direct request from the King, and I agreed to accompany Gawaine to Arthur's court. But, it was not the King that I cared to see, it was Guinevere, the Queen.

Chapter 10

Merlin had shown me ancient scrolls, written in Latin, that tell about the beginning of Londinium, hundreds of years ago, as a Roman settlement. He could not decipher whether it was built first as a military fort or trading center but, in either case, it was located where the river is narrow enough to build a bridge and deep enough for large warships or trading vessels.

The scrolls said that the first Roman building, in what is now called Londinium, was a fort to protect the wooden bridge that had been put across the Thames River as a means of retreat for the Roman army attacking the Britons at Colchester. Within twenty years, soldier's families, tradesmen and foreign merchants developed a civilian settlement outside the defenses of the fort. Soon, it became an important trade port and the most important town in Britain where the Roman governor had his palace.

Londinium was the site of a great battle between the Romans and the famous and revered Queen Boudica who slaughtered the inhabitants, severed the heads of her captives and threw them in the Walbrook River. Then she burned the town to the ground. After she was finally defeated, and the rebellion put down, the Romans rebuilt the town and constructed the Londinium wall for defense around the northern side of the town.

After the Romans left Britain, the barbarians invaded. When they attacked Londinium, the people fled the town rather than stand and fight. The barbarians laid waste to the town, and it was not rebuilt until Vortigern gave the town to Hengist, the Saxon, as payment for driving out the barbarians.

Londinium is once more a British town. Arthur and his armies expelled the Saxons during the seven-year war, and the British language is once again spoken on the town streets. Most of the wall is still intact, and our masons marvel at the breadth and strength of this ancient construction and the skill and knowledge the Romans must have had to build the wall, as well as roads and aqueducts that bring water from the river into the town. The gates, which have been restored, are closed, guarded and patrolled all night.

Arthur's palace was built for Aurelius Ambrosius after he freed Britain from the nightmare of Vortigern and his Saxons. The palace residence has ornate gardens, a large bathhouse, an entrance hall and an assembly hall, where a large number of people can see the King and Queen seated on their thrones on a raised platform.

The palace was comprised of four large wings, forming a square around the garden. Two wings contained rooms built around courtyards, in which the most favored kings and knights had temporary or permanent residence. Another wing contained the King and Queen's private chambers.

But, the place that Arthur loved best in the whole of Britain was his Great Hall.

Two rows of tables and chairs or benches ran the length of the Hall with a wide aisle between the tables and narrower aisles between the tables and the walls. When the nighttime meal was served the King and Queen sat in the center of one of the rows and the kings, barons, knights and their ladies took their places on either side of the King and Queen and across from him, according to their rank or privilege.

The Great Hall is where Arthur and his knights gathered to hear stories of each other's adventures and battles. Although I have not seen it myself, I have heard that knights have ridden their horses through the open doors and stopped before the King to deliver important news or to request some boon or adventure.

In all of my experiences, the Hall was a place of good-fellowship and good eating and drinking. Never would a sword or knife be drawn in anger, as that would mean banishment from the Hall, forever.

The walls were festooned with the shields and banners of the knights who died in Arthur's service. It was deemed a great honor to be recognized this way, and the remembrance of those heroes added to the greatness of the Hall. When everyone was at supper, and there was a joyful noise of knights and warriors eating, drinking and boasting of their deeds and prowess, the hall had an aura of power and mystical destiny that could not be achieved anywhere else in Britain, except at the Giant's Dance at Stonehenge.

There was one seat in the Hall that no one dared sit in. Merlin called it the Siege Perilous, and he warned us that, through magic, it was meant only for the greatest knight in the land: the one without sin, who would find the Christ cup and bring it to heaven. If anyone dared to sit in the seat, he would die a horrible and dishonorable death.

No one has ever admitted to me that he had placed his ass in the Siege Perilous. Nor will I admit to having tried it myself, when no one was watching. But, I do admit that the fact that I am still alive and in good health makes me doubt the truth of Merlin's warning.

When we arrived in Londinium, Gawain took me to his lodgings in King Arthur's palace and made me comfortable and as welcome as an honored brother-in-arms. Then he had me dressed in the finest clothes he had and brought me to where the King and Queen sat side-by-side. Arthur was very pleased to see me.

While the King kept talking on and on about my prowess and courage, and lavished me with praise and honor, which embarrassed me greatly, I remained almost silent through it all, with my eyes cast to the ground. The Queen said not a word but she was in a restive mood and only glanced at me with indifference. Finally, since I acted boorishly and appeared unwilling or unable to speak or converse as a normal person, I was dismissed and free to leave the court and return to Gawain's lodging. From then on, I refused to go anywhere near the King, and I spent my days and nights in miserable solitude.

Finally, one morning, Gawain could ignore my misery no longer.

"Lancelot, my dear companion," he said, "why are you so overcome with sadness? Tell me who troubles you, and I shall take revenge on him, no matter who he is."

"Ah, sir," I answered, "what troubles me cannot be helped by anyone but the one for whom my heart aches. But, if you will, you can do me a great service. All I ask is that you go to court and attend the King and Queen. Then return to me and tell me if anyone talks about or asks about me."

It happened that morning that Gawain returned to Arthur's court, and after breakfast, he and the King and Queen talked about the White Knight. When Gawain stood to leave, the Queen joined him and they walked away from the King.

"Gawain," she said, "I know that you have that good knight in your lodging and that you look after his needs. He is the handsomest youth I have ever seen, but he has neither the courage nor wit to behave as a gentleman and speak with charm and grace. I very much wish to see him and know more about him. I ask that you arrange for me see him."

"My lady," said Gawain, "I do not control him, but I will do all that I can to satisfy your request."

When Gawain returned to his lodgings and found me waiting for him I immediately asked if anyone had mentioned or asked about me.

"My dear friend, the Queen has asked about you, She desires nothing more than to see you. What shall I tell her?"

This was what I had been hoping and waiting for. I began to shake with joy and fear. "Gawain," I said, "I will see the Queen, but you must arrange it so that the court will not know of our meeting and no one will be able to hear what we say to each other."

"Do not worry," said Gawain, smiling, "I shall see to it." Then Gawain returned to the Queen and told her that she would meet the White Knight in a wooded copse, when it was near night.

That evening after supper, Gawain and the Queen went for a stroll in the castle gardens. When they saw that no one was watching, they slipped through a gate and made their way across a small meadow to a nearby stand of leafy trees. It was already beginning to turn dark and I had hidden myself in the shadows. As soon as Gawaine and the Queen sat down on the grass, I approached them and dropped to my knees.

"Madam," said Gawaine as he rose to leave us, "here is the greatest knight I have ever known. I leave him in your care."

It was a cloudless night and the moonlight coming through the trees was enough to light the Queen's face. She looked even more beautiful than I remembered. I felt as if I had lost all control of my senses and I was sure that if she asked a question I would at best, not be able to speak or, at worst, do no more than babble gibberish like a village idiot. I was shaking and I felt the blood drain from my face. The Queen saw my terror, embarrassment and distress and she took pity on me. She stood up lightly, leaned over me, put her hands under my arms and brought me upright and standing close in front of her.

Her hands were still on me as she laughed pleasantly and said, "Sir, you have nothing to fear from me or anyone else for you are a powerful warrior. You have earned great honor by your deeds and we have looked forward eagerly to your presence. If we have failed to make you welcome I beg your forgiveness. Still, it seems as if you have hidden from us in Gawain's lodging. Why have you avoided the King's court? Why are you concealing your identity from me? Now, first tell me, by whom were you made a knight?"

The Queen's closeness should have made me even more anxious and awkward but her hands and her sweet, soft voice calmed me somewhat.

I took a deep breath and answered, "King Arthur knighted me, my lady."

The Queen looked surprised. "When did this happen?"

"My lady, do you not remember the youth who was brought to the King by a lady in white who was richly attended and who also brought two young knights named Lionel and Bors?"

"Ah, yes," said the Queen, "I remember now. You were the young man who demanded to be knighted the next day. Then at the feast you demanded your right to serve the Lady of Nohaut. I heard no more of you after you said farewell to me and left our court. Was it you who sent a very beautiful lady to me who said that the White Knight had defeated her lord?"

"Yes, my lady."

"Were you able to serve the Lady of Nohaut?"

"Yes, my lady."

"Now tell me truthfully, did you overcome the defenses of Dolorous Garde and was it you who freed the knights from Dolorous Prison?"

"Yes, my lady,"

Then the Queen asked a question that made my heart pound and my hands shake.

"You are a very young man. Why did you face such great challenges and perform such wondrous deeds of arms?"

I did not want to answer that question and I hesitated, hoping she would not pursue it.

"You may not ignore me. Answer me and tell me the truth," the Queen demanded. "I promise that no matter what you tell me I shall not reveal your secret. I suspect that I already know the answer. You have risked your life and limb for the love of some lady or damsel. Now tell me who she is, by the obeisance that you owe me."

I lowered my head and answered so quietly that my voice was barely above a whisper. "My lady, your surmise is correct. I have done all that I could for the love of a lady. But that lady is the Queen. My lady, it is you."

"Me?" the Queen exclaimed in surprise.

"Yes, it is true. For you, my lady."

At this, the Queen had to stop to catch her breath and compose herself. "What does this mean?" she asked softly, "Is your love for me so great? How long have you loved me with such devotion?"

"My lady, since the day you made me your friend."

"My friend?" she asked in puzzlement, "and when did I call you my friend?'

"My lady, before I took my leave of the court to begin my journey to Nohaut I came to you and said that I would be your knight. Then you said that you wished me to be your knight and your "friend". Since then, I have never been in such dire straits that I did not remember that word ...friend. That word has comforted me in all my troubles. It has made me forsake the love of all others and released me from burdens unfairly placed upon me. It has fed me when I was hungry and warmed me when I was cold."

Guinevere put her hand on my shoulder and gently pulled me close. Then she tenderly kissed me on my eyes and mouth.

"Dear friend," she whispered, "there is yet one challenge you must overcome for your love of me. You must tell me who you are."

"My lady," I said, almost bursting with happiness and love and pride, "truly, I am of great and noble birth. The name given to me when I was born was Galahad. My mother was a Queen in Brittany, the Lady Helen. My father was a great and noble knight and puissant King in Brittany. I am called Lancelot of the Lake but I am King Ban's son of Benoic."

We talked for a while longer, but I do not remember what was said. Then one of the Queen's ladies came for her, and she left me with a long kiss on the mouth. I do not know how I was able to return to Gawain without dying of joy.

The next day, I went to court where I made my name and heritage known to all. And it was with great pomp and ceremony that King Arthur made Sir Lancelot a knight of his own court.

Chapter 11

The days went by slowly as my lord Lancelot worked as he was accustomed to and performed the tasks that were his responsibility. I used the days to transcribe my hastily scribbled notes and to record my fresh recollections on clean pages. It was after the evening meal that Sir Lancelot had time to sit next to me and tell me of his life and battles. But I was interested in more than that and one evening I asked him to tell me as much as he would about King Arthur, Queen Guinevere, the knights he had known, and most of all, the Wizard Merlin.

"Master Lonmarch," said Sir Lancelot with a sly smile, "I am confident that you have already heard much about those illustrious personages but I would wager that you have not heard the truth about them. Since you are my scribe and the written word must be true I shall also make you the judge of the veracity of my tale."

Although I had not yet met him, I knew who Merlin was. I was puzzled, yet pleased, when I noticed him watching me and smiling with quiet satisfaction.

It was during the winter months in London that I came to know and understand Merlin better than those closest to him, except for Arthur. By the time I met him, he was a very old man who had lived an amazing and exciting life. I was the only young person who was truly interested in him and unafraid of him. He often sought me out, and we would spend an afternoon in some private nook while he told me about Britain before the coming of Constantine and about anyone and anything I was interested in. But though he was a storyteller, he was much more than that to me. He was also a sincere and trustworthy listener to whom I often unburdened myself.

Merlin was just a young boy when Vortigern forced him to prophesy his future. The despised king of Britain had been advised by his priests to find a "Cambion," which is a child born of a human mother and a fiend of the devil for a father. I think I know how Merlin came to have such an evil and frightening birthright. His mother was a noblewoman, but his father was unnamed. There was nothing unusual in a lady having a child out of wedlock, so that could not be the origin of Merlin's devilish origin. I believe that Merlin himself created the myth because he was a frail child who needed a defense against the brutish contemporaries in his life.

In fact, Merlin was never strong or sturdy. Yet, no one else but Merlin has been close to three British kings without ever couching a lance or wielding a sword. First, when Aurelius Ambrosius returned to Britain from Brittany, he became Ambrosius' closest friend and councilor. After Ambrosius' death, he disappeared for a while, until he was summoned to become Uther's "magician." And, of course, he has been "kingmaker" and foster father to Arthur.

Most people believed that Merlin was a wizard and necromancer. I am not one of those superstitious fools. But, I do believe that he was very clever and far seeing. He used the weaknesses of people to his own advantage. He used fear and weakly held faith to enhance his own so-called magical powers. He lied and exaggerated and made up stories hinting at his powers, so that people were in awe or afraid of him.

I believe that Merlin wore his "magical powers" as a suit of armor to protect him, not only from violence, but, also, from those who sought to separate him from the King, so that they could weaken his influence and strengthen their own.

Any thinking man would be right to doubt Merlin's powers, but there is a difference between doubt and knowledge. No one knew that Merlin had no magic, and my friend did nothing to ease the doubt.

New stories about Merlin kept rising from the mists of fear and superstition. The stories were and still are widely believed. They were spread quickly by common folk, but the nobility also accepted them as truth. Even the priests and bishops of the new religion feared his "evil eye" and hid behind the rood when they crossed his path. The priests of the old religion did not exactly fear him, but they did not deny his powers either.

Merlin, the magician, is credited with finding a giant to help him build the "Giant's Dance" as a burial place for Ambrosius. He is said to have been able to change his form into anyone or anything. He has been seen as a woodcutter, carrying an ax hung around his head. He has been seen as an ugly forester, driving a herd of deer. He is said to have appeared to Arthur as a handsome man, then a beautiful boy and then as a peasant. He has been seen as a hunchback, who carries a club and drives beasts in front of him.

The story of Arthur's conception is a good example of Merlin's manipulation of the truth. No one can truly know who Arthur's father really was. Yet, it is widely believed that Merlin cast a spell on Uther to make him appear as the Duke of Cornwall so that he could get between Ygraine's legs.

Merlin laughs every time he hears that story.

One day he said to me, "Listen, Lancelot, there are only three truths to that story. First, the guards at

Tintagel were generously bribed. Second, Ygraine was not as virtuous as generally believed. Besides, Uther was twenty years younger than Gorlois and had a reputation for skill and stamina in the bedchamber, while Gorlois had one foot in the grave. Third, why would a beautiful, young and vivacious lady be satisfied with being the Queen of a pile of rocks called Cornwall, when she could be the High Queen of Londinium, Westminster and everywhere else in Britain?"

Nothing sealed belief in Merlin's wizardry more than the story about how Arthur obtained the sword Excalibur. It had to be a miracle or magic to explain how a Lady appeared out of a lake, at Merlin's behest, and offered the sword and its scabbard to Arthur. Even I might have believed that some magic was involved if Merlin had not confessed to me that two boats were involved, and that the Lady of the Lake was none other than my Lady Niniane and Merlin's favorite accomplice in all things magical.

Merlin always seemed to be amused by something and sometimes, he would break out into laughter when no one else noticed anything funny. But, there was always an underlying sadness about him. Some of the things he told me, made me think that he felt that he had failed in some great endeavor. Sometimes a look of great weariness came over him when Arthur appeared. He always watched the King as if his eyes were locked on him. That stare made me uncomfortable, as I had no idea how Merlin really felt about the King.

As I spent more and more time with the old man, I began to realize that he only cared about two people in the world ... Arthur and me. He seemed to have a genuine liking for me, although that may have been because of my relation to Niniane. At any rate, I suppose that I began to think of him as part of my small family. As I thought of Niniane as my mother, I thought of Merlin as my grandfather. Never a cross word passed between us, and I always felt that any confidence I shared with him would be kept our secret.

In the short time I had been at Arthur's court, Merlin seemed to age rapidly, and he had more and more difficulty getting around during cold weather. He complained about the cold, and I was always diligent about wrapping him from head to toe in fur blankets.

He seemed to be hanging on to life for some great event to happen. Finally, one day, I overcame my good manners and good sense and asked him if he was afraid of death.

Merlin smiled at me and put his gnarled hand on mine.

"No, Lancelot, I am not afraid of death. I have lived long enough and my time is almost over. But, there is one more miracle that I wish to see before I die."

"What is that, my dear friend?" I asked.

"I am waiting for the birth of the Knight of the Holy Grail. When I hear that the savior of Britain is born, I will go to sleep."

"Merlin, tell me, who will that knight be? How will we know him? Who is his father?"

"You will see, Lancelot. You will see."

No matter how much I begged and pleaded, all he would say was, "You will see, Lancelot. You will see."

Uther's lust for Ygraine did not last long after their marriage, which took place thirteen days after Gorlois, the Duke of Cornwall, was sent to his ancestors on a giant funeral pyre. With a new ring on her finger, and a larger diadem on her head, Ygraine became the center of attention at court. But, for Uther, Ygraine was now a possession and no longer a desire. He ignored her, and she was generally free to follow her own interests until, at three months, her pregnancy became obvious to the court.

The impending birth of a son and heir piqued Uther's interest in the Queen and her comfort and wellbeing became important to him. When the healthy boy was born, Uther demonstrated his pride and delight by holding a series of feasts and tournaments and distributing generous gifts to the kings and knights of the court and coins to the common folk and the poor.

The baby boy was named Arthur.

The crown did not sit securely or peacefully on Uther's head. Kings and knights, who had sworn fealty, continued their intrigues against him. There were plots and cabals and shifting alliances intended to depose the king and set a rival on the throne in his stead. Uther was confident in his ability to thwart the dangers to his own safety, but he was more cautious and concerned about the safety of his child. As a precaution, he took the prudent step of bringing Merlin to court and giving him the responsibility for the child's safety as his guardian and protector against all evil, human and otherwise.

Arthur spent the first six years of his life in his father's court, where he was pampered and spoiled and where he learned the advantages of being the High King's son. Uther made sure that he would not learn humility or caution for the power he would one day inherit. Instead, he was taught to relish power, and he learned arrogance and pride. Arthur grew to believe that his future kingship was his by right, and that he had no duty or obligation to anyone or anything but his kingdom.

Ygraine died of a fever when Arthur was six years old. It did not seem a great loss to the boy, since his mother had shown little interest in him from the time of his birth. Merlin had been his closest adult companion and surrogate parent and, therefore, the only one to ever earn a tender thought from the boy.

The next year Arthur began his training for knighthood. With Merlin continuing his role of protector, Arthur was sent to the estate of Sir Ector de Maris, one of Uther's most reliable allies and a knight of great fame and repute. Sir Ector owned lands in the northeast, which Uther deemed far enough from the plots and intrigues of Londinium. He and his pleasant wife had one son, Cai, who was two years older than Arthur and already well into his training for knighthood as a page to one of Ector's knights.

Life as a page was a difficult time for Arthur who, until then, had led an indulgent life. He resented the menial tasks and subordination to a lowly knight, and he fought constantly with Cai until his first experience with weapons training.

Even at this tender age, Arthur showed that his only interest was fighting and war. He was the first page at the Pell and the last one to leave it. He rode the ponies the hardest and put them through the most difficult maneuvers, never caring about falls, cuts and bruises. In mock battles with Cai and the other pages, he attacked with fierce determination, and often had to be pulled away from opponents to avoid their serious injury. The other pages tried to change his behavior by attacking him as a group and beating him, but being held down and pummeled had no effect. His vicious behavior continued until Sir Ector intervened with threats that he would be sent back to his father. That was enough to quiet Arthur down, but it did not ease the unexplainable anger and urge in him to fight and destroy. His behavior towards the other pages became more civil, but he made no friends among them, and only Cai was part of his later life.

Arthur was a thirteen year old squire when word came to Sir Ector of King Uther's death, supposedly by poisoning but more likely from a war wound that continued to fester in spite of the best efforts of all sorts of healers.

Before dying, Uther had named the Archbishop of Canterbury as Regent of Britain, to rule until Arthur was old enough to be knighted and take the crown. But, the desire for power burned hot in every king and baron, and Britain was wracked by chaos and war. Alliances formed and broke apart, as the more powerful antagonists sought to gain the crown by force of arms or by connivance and murder.

Three years of anarchy passed. Arthur had completed his training as a squire and was at the age when he could be knighted and crowned king. A council had been formed to assure Arthur's ascension to the throne and the restoration of unity to Britain. The Archbishop of Canterbury, Sir Baudwin, Sir Ulfius, Sir Brastian, Sir Ector and, of course, Merlin, comprised the council.

There was no doubt that bringing Arthur forward to claim his rights would be fraught with danger. The kings and barons, all committed to their own advancement, would oppose the boy in every conceivable way including casting doubt on the legitimacy of his birth.

In fact, anyone who had known Uther Pendragon as a young man might doubt that Arthur was his natural born son. Uther was below average height, unusually broad and strong with wavy black hair and swarthy skin. But what people remarked most about him were his cold, black, penetrating eyes and the perpetual condescending sneer on his lips. Arthur was of average height and fair skinned with light brown hair, unlike both Uther and the Duke of Cornwall. Those who knew Merlin before he was old and white-haired say that he was fair and had light brown hair.

Uther had done much before his death to establish the legitimacy of his son, and for many of the kings and barons who supported him, Arthur's rights were never an issue. But those who sought the throne for themselves, used the legitimacy issue to gain support, from among those who were not committed either way.

In order to defeat this attack, the council decided that Arthur's claim had to be reinforced by some supernatural act that no one could argue about or deny. They left the details of providing such a magical endorsement to Merlin.

As usual, the great charlatan performed a masterful illusion followed by widespread exaggeration. He produced a large boulder with a sword sticking out of it. The Archbishop announced that only the rightful King of Britain would be able to withdraw the sword from the stone. No one knew that the stone had a crack in it and that the sword was merely stuck in the crack rather than penetrating the stone. Baudwin, Ulfius, Brastias, Ector and his son, Cai, were all asked to pull the sword free. Of course, despite heroic efforts, they all failed.

Then Arthur came forward and easily, but dramatically, retrieved the sword. The gullible peasants and townsmen who were invited to witness the miracle were suitably impressed and convinced. They could be relied upon to spread the word and increase the magnificence of the miracle by retelling it again and again.

The Saxons, who had, for the most part, been brought under control by Uther, took advantage of his death and Britain's internal conflict to further their own gains. It was not long before the land returned to death and destruction under the German sword and firebrand.

As soon as Arthur came to the throne, he swore to rid Britain of the Saxon menace and set out to attack the Anglian stronghold at York. The Saxon leader, Colgrin, gathered an alliance of Saxons, Scots and Picts and marched south to meet him. They fought at the River Douglas where Arthur and his forces were victorious, despite heavy losses. Colgin and his surviving forces retreated to York where they were besieged by Arthur's allies. The siege was soon lifted without the Saxon's defeat.

Arthur fought twelve battles against the Saxons, but they were not finally overcome until the last battle which took place at Badon Hill near Wiltshire.

Arthur's spies had learned where the Saxon troops were on the march. The British set an ambush on the Saxon column. The Saxons pulled into a line of warriors standing shoulder-to-shoulder with their shields locked together along the roadway and fought desperately until sundown, when their chief withdrew his battered troops to a nearby hilltop under cover of darkness.

The next morning, Arthur's men were rested and well fed, while the Saxons had spent the night on a steep, exposed hilltop without food, water or firewood. As usual, Arthur was impatient and generous with the expenditure of his men's lives. Rather than starving the trapped Saxons into submission, he ordered his forces to charge up the hill.

Both sides engaged in a fierce battle throughout the day, with the Britons charging up the hill and the Saxons countercharging down it. The battle finally ended late in the day, when Arthur led a charge up the steep slope and broke the Saxon shieldwall. The Saxons fled down the hill with the Britons chasing and slaughtering them, until it was too dark to continue.

The battle of Badon Hill was the last major battle fought against the Saxons, and they have not threatened Britain again until now.

Many kings and barons were unconvinced by the so-called miracle of Arthur drawing the sword from the stone or they chose to ignore it. Arthur's crowning was followed by a terrible civil war led by King Lot. In all, eleven kings fought against Arthur. Peace and unity did not come to Britain until my father, King Ban and my uncle, King Bohort, came from Brittany with their best knights to fight for Arthur of Britain.

I find it interesting that the Bretons saved Britain for Arthur. After all, Constantine saved Britain, and he was a Breton. And I am a Breton who is supposed to save Britain by finding Jesus' cup. I also find it amusing that Arthur is the grandson of a Breton.

By the time Arthur had achieved the accolade of High King, he had spent the better part of his life in the saddle with a sword in his hand fighting the Saxons and his own jealous countrymen. Nevertheless, he had dismounted often enough to leave a string of bastards across the countryside, and he relished his way of life.

It was Merlin who insisted to Arthur that he could not continue living the life of a soldier forever, and that he had to secure Britain's future by leaving a legitimate heir. After Merlin's assurance that he could continue to spill his seed where he wished, Arthur agreed to marry Guinevere, the young daughter of King Leodegrance, one of Arthur's staunchest political and military supporters.

For some reason, which he never explained to me, Merlin disapproved of Guinevere. Nevertheless, she was a good choice for Arthur. Leodegrance deserved the honor. The fifteen-year-old maiden was exceptionally pretty, and there was every expectation that she would produce heirs for the kingdom.

Whether Merlin tutored him or not, Arthur was an astute politician with a very flexible sense of honor and duty. He set knight against knight and king against king, and whenever there was a choice to be made of which side to take, he always took the side that would benefit him. As a king and a man, he was little trusted, but hundreds of knights loved him and swore oaths to defend his rights and his person to the death.

My relationship with Arthur became strained after I learned all about my father. Arthur only spoke about how my father and uncle had answered his plea for help, but he downplayed their roles in ending the civil wars.

I think that Arthur's feelings toward me were mixed. I was the one that he sent out to beat rebellious kings and barons into submission. When a champion was needed, for one reason or another, I am the one he sent into battle. I was always the one to defend the

King's rights against any and all who defied him. Yet I think that his guilt ate at him, and he plotted ways to shame me or humble me and bring me down from the lofty heights of honor bestowed on me by his court. I think that he would have been glad for any hurt I suffered, short of death.

Nevertheless, I was Arthur's man. I had sworn fealty to him, but there were times when it was extremely difficult to remain faithful to him. I wanted to kill him when he betrayed Tristan and befriended King Mark. I think that I would have ripped out his throat and taken Guinevere away with me, if she had not stopped me.

When I first saw the Queen, I was almost seventeen years old and she was a bare three years older than me. I was still a child, in spite of my man's body, but I was old enough to fall completely and desperately in love with the most beautiful and desirable woman I had ever seen.

I still remember what she wore, and how she looked, when I saw her before leaving for Nohaut. She was dressed in a long, light blue gown in the style of the Roman women of earlier days. She was slim, but shapely, and the gown was very tight around her waist and bodice so that her breasts were accentuated and partly uncovered. A fur-trimmed cape covered her bare shoulders and gold bracelets circled her arms and her wrists. Her long black hair, which curled slightly, fell down her back and forward over her shoulders. Her bright and clear blue eyes in a pale oval face were shadowed with kohl and her full lips were tinged with red. I could not take my eyes off her, I felt myself shake and my knees weaken. If it had not been for Gawain standing next to me, I would have fallen.

When next I saw the Queen, I was twenty years old. I had grown even bigger and stronger over the past three years. I was a full-grown man who had killed many men and been tempted in many ways. Nevertheless, when I saw Guinevere again, I was still a child.

At the time of their marriage, Arthur was more than twenty years her senior. At first, the girl was thrilled with the idea of being Queen of all the British, and she set aside any concerns she had about the difference in ages. Besides, many good marriages had been made between older men and young maids, such as between Gorlois and Arthur's mother, Ygraine. In addition, Arthur had a lusty reputation and he had left royal by-blow throughout the country. So, Guinevere convinced herself that her marriage would be fulfilling, and that it would not be long before she was the mother of the next High King of Britain.

Unfortunately, circumstances did not work out well for Guinevere. Arthur did not intend to alter his way of life. He gave no thought to the needs of a young wife who was inexperienced in the royal ways of the world. He managed to avoid his marital duties as much as possible by riding off to every rumored Saxon incursion or, when there was no one to fight, going off on hunting trips with his cronies.

When he returned to Londinium, after being away for weeks or months, there was drunken carousing, jousting and feasting and, under the influence of some of his favorite knights, he continued his old ways of whoring in the inns and taverns of town. Only occasionally was the Queen called to the King's bedchamber where she found no love, compassion or friendship, only rough and brief coupling.

It was difficult at first for me to understand Arthur's growing dislike (if not outright hatred) for his Queen. The one subject Guinevere would not discuss with me, even in private, was her relationship with her husband.

It was well known that Arthur had fathered children all over the country of Britain. But that was when he was a much younger man. Reports of his prowess under the bedcovers, starting to peter out, had already started by the time of the marriage. Nevertheless, as time went by, Guinevere's failure to become pregnant was blamed on her infertility, with never a thought given to the possibility of the King's impotence.

Whatever the cause, Arthur grew to resent the Queen. He stopped calling her to his bedchamber, and he began to show his displeasure at her being around him in public. Guinevere was frightened for her life, as there were many examples of unloved Queens being beheaded by their king. Arthur's public displays of indifference embittered the Queen and encouraged her enemies. Her defense was to put on a public face of merriment and unconcern for her husband's dishonorable behavior.

When she was falsely accused of infidelity and treason, she gathered what allies she could to defend her against her accusers on the field of battle. Those who were loyal to her were constantly on the alert to the dangers of rumors and innuendos. The threat of beheading, burning at the stake or branding was a constant background to her daily existence.

Guinevere's hopes and natural optimism eventually turned to anger and despair, and then to plans for revenge against the king and his cronies for their disrespect and abandonment. By the time I arrived in Arthur's court, the Queen had already formed some liaisons that offered her a small measure of power and influence and some passion for her bed. But, I changed everything for her.

When I returned from Dolorous Garde, and she learned who I was, understood what I had done for her. and the extent of my devotion, her attitude toward me changed. From all the talk she heard about me, there was no doubt that no other knight, even Gawain, could match my prowess in battle. The ladies of the court lost no time throwing themselves at me, and word must have gotten back to her that I would have no liaisons.

For the first time in her life, Guinevere had an invincible champion who would fight and kill any and all of her enemies without qualms or hesitation. The only problem she had was that for the first time in her life, she was also in love.

At the holiday feasts and celebrations, Guinevere and I were almost inseparable. Arthur beamed when I danced with the Queen or sat at her feet as Kings, knights and their ladies paid court to her.

The Queen, however, was my own special curse. She had many favorites among the knights and she may, or may not, have been carrying on affairs with them. But in public, she treated me as if I was her favorite puppy. She kissed my cheeks and hugged me. She fondled and petted me. She whispered in my ear and flirted with me in front of everyone. Yet, her carousing with the boy-knight raised no suspicion and was seen by everyone, including Arthur, as harmless fun.

I know that I was a handsome man both because I am the son of King Ban and because I was the object of desire of so many ladies since Nohaut. Furthermore, I had not one single scar on my face or body despite all of the battles I had fought. In private, her behavior towards me was much different. She arranged to have us alone together as often as possible. With no one to watch us, she would remove her outer garments and leave on only a thin shift so that her private parts were only barely concealed. She kissed me passionately on the lips over and over. She held me close, moved her body wantonly against me, and touched me in ways that sent shivers through my body, all the while whispering that she loved me and wanted me. She drew me to the bed and came on top of me, but pushed my hands away whenever I tried to touch her.

Her behavior towards me was hot or cold by turns. She would refuse to see me for days and then, when she finally let me near her, she would accuse me of ignoring her. She teased me and coyly hinted at lying with me, then laughed at my embarrassment and struggles with myself. She tested me repeatedly. She put me in compromising situations with her prettiest ladies in waiting, who were told to tempt me. I had to prove my unyielding devotion to her by resisting every temptation offered to me.

Guinevere played with me while I burned with love and lust. Between her and the ladies of the court, there was no relief for me, and there were times when I yearned to kill every knight in sight, or at least to be killed and be put out of my misery.

Chapter 12

At first, I was confused by Arthur's relationships with the Barons of Orkney and with their mother, his half-sister, Morgause. It was not long, however, before the reasons for their status as the King's favorites became obvious to me.

Morgause was the only child, a daughter, of Gorloise, the Duke of Cornwall, and his young wife, Ygraine. She was barely three years old when her half-brother, Arthur, was born to her mother and Uther, the High King of Britain.

Lot, the King of Lothian, had been a long-time supporter and ally of Uther. When Morgause reached sixteen years of age, Uther gave her in marriage to King Lot as a reward for his loyalty and allegiance and to strengthen their mutual interests through family bonds. At least that was the commonly held opinion. I think that he wanted Morgause out of his household and out of his sight. She looked like her father, and was a constant reminder of Gorloise and whatever role Arthur might have had in his death. She also made no secret of her hatred for Arthur, which grew stronger as she grew older and understood the ways of the world. She looked at him with the most malevolent stare, which made him uneasy just at the sight of her.

When Morgause was only seven months married to Lot, she gave birth to a son she named Mordaunt. Lot knew that the child was not his, and when his wife confessed that Arthur had raped her, his desire for retribution knew no bounds. Morgause had always had a reputation for being clever and ambitious, and her marriage to old King Lot was her choice no matter what anyone says. By the time they were married, he was totally enamored and easily manipulated (some say bewitched) by her in all matters of governance, war and peace, and, in all likelihood, in matters of the bedchamber. Still, for all of her hate, Morgause could not influence King Lot against Uther. But, when Uther died a few months after Mordaunt's birth, all of Lot's vows of loyalty and fealty died with him, and he was free to take his revenge against Uther's son.

For the next fourteen years, Lot was the leader of the kings and barons who opposed Arthur's kingship and fought against him. Even after the great battles in which my father and uncle helped Arthur achieve many victories, Lot continued to resist and lead his armies to war and refused to surrender and swear fealty.

During those years, while Lot fought Arthur, Morgause gave birth to four more sons: Agravaine, Gawain, Gaheris and the youngest, Gareth, who was born as Lot lay mortally ill.

After Lot was dead, Morgause brought her four eldest sons to Arthur's court. She said she wanted Arthur to make peace with his nephews and to knight them when they came of age but she had a more sinister plan for the future. Arthur was more than happy to welcome his sister and her family, now that Lot was gone and his nephew's presence at court would guaranty the loyalty of Lothian.

Morgause was always welcome at Arthur's court and he deferred to her and showed her more respect and consideration than he showed his own Queen.

The sons of Lot were as different as day and night. What more can be said of Mordaunt than he was adept at avoiding battle and never took part in jousting or tournaments. He took great care of his safety and well-being. Those who could do sums (like myself) believed that Mordaunt was in the womb before Morgause married Lot. If that was true, who would be the likely candidate for fatherhood?

The black-hearted coward had a different relationship with Arthur than anyone else. There was no love between them, but not even Merlin was closer to the King. He was the most powerful and influential member of Arthur's various councils. His arguments almost always held sway with Arthur, whether the matter was land distribution and acquisition, trade agreements, construction of towns, bridges, forts, roads or anything else. He was also the authority on matters of levying armies, taxation, war, and peace agreements. Perhaps most importantly, a poor knight seeking a fief from the King, in return for service, had to first satisfy Mordaunt of his worthiness.

There is no doubt in anyone's mind that Mordaunt sought to be the next King. He did nothing to squelch rumors to that effect and he may even have advanced them. No one seemed to care that Mordaunt might be illegitimate. It would not be as if Arthur had lain with some country girl or milkmaid. There was royalty on both sides of Mordaunt and that was enough to assuage any public or religious concern about incest.

As things stood, if Arthur died suddenly, Mordaunt would be named King by acclamation. His first act would be to murder Guinevere. I would have to leave Britain and return to Brittany with my cousins. My liegemen would probably come with me, and many other honorable knights would leave Britain as well.

Agravaine and Gaheris were, from childhood, close to Mordaunt in spite of being physically and emotionally different from him. Both were quick to anger and easily affronted by even the slightest imagined insult. They took their royal birth as a license to be arrogant bullies. If any one of the three brothers made an enemy, the other two took on that enemy as well.

Unlike Mordaunt, Agravaine and Gaheris were quick to draw their swords. In tournaments they fought as one, their favorite tactic being an attack on a single knight from the front and the rear. On the rare occasions, when I fought in a melee, I was always careful to be aware of where the two of them lurked, waiting to select a victim. I would not let either of them out of my sight for more than a few moments.

Arthur would allow no criticism or complaint about his nephews, and that reinforced their dishonorable behavior. There was no love between those two and the king. Nevertheless, Arthur condoned their bad behavior and made excuses for them. No one of high honor and reputation liked the brothers, but they drew other malcontents and low-lives to them like shit draws flies. They were always at the center of some conspiracy and were bent on causing troubles for whoever was the current or on-going favorite of the king.

Then there was Gawain. When I came to Arthur to be knighted, Gawain was already twenty-three years old and the greatest knight in Arthur's court. Although he looked like Agravaine and Gaheris, everything I have said about his brothers was the opposite truth for Gawaine. Finally, there was the young Gareth who was tall, strong as a bull and beautiful of body and spirit. It is still very hard for me to accept that he had the same father as the other four.

Gawain was Arthur's favorite because, well, because he was Gawain. His prowess, courage and loyalty exceeded that of almost all other knights. He was friendly, garrulous. loyal and reliable. He would fight anyone to the death at a word from his uncle. He was a boon companion in a hunting camp, in a tavern and in a whorehouse. He would keep a secret and give you the best advice he could on everything from war to love. There is no doubt that Arthur and Gawain loved each other as father and son.

Of all of the knights in Britain, Gawaine was one of the biggest, strongest, most courageous and most honorable I had ever met. From the very first, he and I were like brothers, and he looked out for my reputation and my interests. His brothers were Guinevere's implacable enemies, but Gawain stood by the Queen. After I returned to Londinium from Joyous Garde, it was understood that if I could not defend the Queen, he would do it in my place.

For me Gawaine was the very model of a chivalrous knight. I believed that there would never be an honorable battle or cause that he would turn his back on. He was slow to anger, but once beyond the point of forgiveness, he would not stop until he had his justice. Unlike his brothers, his love and loyalty towards Arthur was genuine and unquestionable. He was proud and satisfied to be the nephew of the King and he had no greater ambition than to defend Arthur's throne.

My brother-in-arms, Gawain, had only one great weakness that sometimes got him into trouble with a husband or brother. But then nothing could spur him to defend someone's virtue or rights faster than a plea from a beautiful and grateful lady. Unfortunately, there were times when some poor knight he beat into submission at the request of the lovely lady was, in fact, the aggrieved and innocent party.

For all of Gawain's devotion to Arthur, I noticed that, as the years went by, the King spent more time in private conversation with the great knight's three despicable brothers. It finally became obvious to me that the King wanted to be free of Guinevere and that the brothers would do what they could to satisfy him.

I also came to understand that the brothers' support for the King's ambition regarding the Queen was not driven by their love for their uncle but rather their own self-interest in avoiding a chance pregnancy that would place another heir between Mordaunt and the throne. My presence at court heightened their concern because they were not completely sure of Guinevere's barrenness, and they were convinced that our public flirting covered a real love in private. I suspect they feared that Arthur would be forced to accept my child with Guinevere, if we had one, as his own legitimate heir.

Without a public accusation of the Queen's misbehavior or infidelity, there was nothing that I could do to defend her. There were many times when I struggled with the overwhelming desire to kill the bastards of Lothian, but they gave me no honorable excuse to give in to my urges and instinct. What's more, I feared the loss of Gawain's friendship if I harmed his brothers. All I could do was watch and wait for an opportunity to do them harm.

Mordaunt was far and away the shrewdest and most sinister of the three conniving brothers. I am sure that he was the one who hatched most (if not all) of the plots to discredit Guinevere. But, he was very careful to avoid being identified as the instigator of any rumor or accusation of scandal. When asked his opinion of the truth of such calumnies, he was the soul of caution and would neither confirm nor deny any knowledge or express any opinion one way or the other.

Agravaine, being more gullible than Gaheris, was often the tool with which Mordaunt built his lies. The brothers were careful not to include Gawain in any of their accusations of Guinevere's infidelities, but they spread rumors involving many other knights of low rank. When I came to court with all of my innocence and naiveté, I became an immediate target for them.

It took a while for me to understand the workings of the court and the intrigues within and around it. Fortunately, I had friends who looked out for me, including Yvain and Gawain. I also had Merlin who, in addition to being a fount of information, taught me to look beyond the obvious of every issue and to be suspicious of everyone's motives and feigned innocence.

With the first hint of an affair between the Queen and me, I became furious over the insult to my honor, but Lionel and Bors were the cooler heads who calmed me down and helped me to realize that I needed to direct my anger only at those who were the initiators of such scurrilous falsehoods.

It did not take much time or effort to learn that Agravaine was the one who needed to learn the danger of offending me. Once he was made an example of, and punished severely, others would be unlikely to involve themselves in matters affecting my reputation and honor.

It was my practice at court to wear a woolen shirt and linen trousers covered with a linen tunic. I began to wear a light mail vest between the shirt and tunic. I carried no weapon and had only a small dirk that I used at meals.

For several days, I watched the comings and goings of the three brothers. The first time I saw them together, heading towards Mordaunt's quarters, I followed them. As soon as they had entered and closed the door behind them, I rushed up and beat on the door with the side of my fist.

A page opened the door a crack and I struck it hard with my shoulder, bursting it wide open and throwing the page across the room. I took three steps into the room. The three brothers needed only a quick glance to recognize the threat that faced them. Mordaunt lurched for a corner of the room and dove behind a heavy wooden desk. Agravaine ran towards a sword that stood propped up against a wall opposite to where he was standing. Gaheris stood as still as a statue directly in front of me. The look of surprise on his face turned instantly into blind hate.

I surged into Gaheris' body, grabbed his throat with both of my hands and, shoving him off balance, drove him across the room and into Agravaine, who was bent over reaching for the sword. I dropped Gaheris, whose eyes appeared to be popping out of his head, and turned my attention to Agravaine, who was trying to scramble away and get to his feet so that he could use the sword. I kicked him in his side as hard as I could and he howled. I picked him up off his knees with my hands under his armpits, lifted him off the floor and slammed his back into the wall, over and over. He looked at me with no expression on his face, as if he knew he was going to die. I growled at him and with just the strength in my hands and arms, I turned and threw him half way across the room where he crumpled to the floor without a sound.

As Agravaine landed in a heap, I felt a sting in my back. I turned and saw Mordaunt in an odd sort of twisted crouch holding my dirk in his hand. I had mistakenly relied on Mordaunt's cowardice, but there he stood, ready to defend himself.

"Stand up, " I growled, " You are a miserable creature, and if you were not Arthur's nephew, I would strangle you on the spot. But, I warn you, should anyone spread any more false rumors about me and the Queen, I will kill you and your brothers, nephews or not. And be sure of this; you will not die honorably by the sword. I will choke the life out of you with my hands as befits the low lives that you are."

Then I left the room.

When I returned to my own lodging, I removed the chain mail vest and found the dented link that had blocked Mordaunt's knife thrust. I was learning that "discretion is the better part of valor."

I stayed in London all winter in defiance of Niniane's instructions but confident enough that the honors heaped upon me had been earned and not a gift bestowed on my father's son.

Arthur and his closest advisors spent their days concerned with governance of the country and military affairs. The King received visitors and ambassadors from other countries. He heard petitions from royals and common folk and meted out civil decisions and justice for outlaws. He dealt with reports of incursions, invasions and acts of treason against the King's law. The priests and holy men hounded him constantly, demanding churches, gold for their churches and more holy days for fasting and penance, which usually required the purchase of forgiveness for sins with gold.

I did not partake in any of the governance activities of Arthur's inner circle, but Merlin did and as I had frequent access to his reflections and thoughts, I began to perceive the deeper and underlying reasons for what I casually observed.

For most knights in Arthur's court, days were taken up with training and exercises including jousting, swordplay, wrestling and all manner of competition involving strength of body and prowess with arms. But there was also a busy round of tournaments, feasts, social gatherings and affairs. Kings and barons came and went with the seasons, since they had to manage their own lands. But, there were many knights who left those obligations to their seneschals and remained at court year round, so that they could enjoy Arthur's boundless generosity.

In earlier times, knights jousted with rounded lance points and covered swords. But, Arthur's knights rebelled against such cowardly practices, and the King relented and allowed jousts to proceed with pointed lances and naked sword blades.

Whether or not blunted weapons were used, there were always many jousting and tournament injuries. Most often, there were bruised or cracked ribs caused by the impact of a lance. There were also broken bones and broken necks, especially when a horse fell over onto its rider.

After jousting or tournaments, a feast was always held in Arthur's Great Hall. The excitement and the rivalries threatened to continue under the King's roof and tempers grew hot, but Arthur's presence always proved enough to prevent jealousy or anger from ruining the night.

The excitement of the occasion and feelings of celebration and good cheer were the responsibility of the minstrels and troubadours, who sang both songs of war and victories and songs of love and loyal devotion. The exploits of knights, past and present, were often sung, much to my chagrin, when I was the subject of their song. The minstrels were handsomely rewarded. Arthur retained them in his household, and even itinerant minstrels were welcomed into the hall, especially at the time of knighting ceremonies.

Sometimes, especially when numbers of squires were gaining their knighthood, the feast would go on for days. Roasted beef, mutton, and pork were served in great quantities. Roasted geese, swan, capon and duck crowded the tables. Fish was also served, with lampreys being a favorite dish. In addition, there was bread, vegetables and fruits, including pears, apples, plums and quince.

It did not take me long to see that the court was rife with immorality. Married ladies, maids and maidens carried on their affairs with knights, princes, kings and squires without a care for privacy or decency on the part of either gender.

Almost all the knights I knew had broken their vows of knighthood. They were disloyal and dishonorable. They fornicated and were unfaithful as husbands. They lived lives devoted to pleasure and greed. The worst of them were guilty of whoring and murder, and I heard some of them brag about how many maidens they had seduced and how many men they had killed.

They cared nothing for the widows and orphans they were sworn to protect. When a squire of noble blood receives the accolade and becomes a knight, the young man gains recognition of his nobility and his right to bear arms. But he, in turn, accepts his obligation to behave morally and loyally to his lord, his brother knights and the common folk of his country.

I was not a monk, nor was I made of stone and unable to feel. The constant and unabashed advances of the young ladies of the court almost drove me mad. They teased me constantly. They touched me and rubbed up against me every chance they got. They flirted, suggested, and tried every temptation and scheme to get me into their beds. Their shameless mothers offered every inducement imaginable (sometimes even themselves) to get me to lay with their daughters. They were so desperate that just having Lancelot's bastard child would satisfy them.

In spite of my caution, there were always rumors of my having lain with some maiden or other. For that reason, I tried to have a witness to all of my comings and goings. Lionel and Bors were my most usual companions, much to their dismay and annoyance, since they were normal men and had their own affairs to look to. Sometimes Yvain would accompany me and, if Gawaine were not on some licentious mission, he would serve as my chaperone.

In sum, life at court was too fraught with intrigue and seduction for me to tolerate longer than the worst winter months. With the first signs of spring, I left Londinium and went searching for peace, quiet and adventure.

The first knights that I encountered shortly after leaving Londinium were especially unfortunate, as they withstood the worst of my accumulated frustrations. Some of them were lucky to escape with their lives.

Chapter 13

An honorable knight, who is aware of his own great prowess, has no need to brag or boast of it. Nevertheless, knights of such repute seem to find each other's company appealing and they form friendships between brother knights that are different from other friendships. That is the way it was between Sir Lamorak, Sir Tristan and me. Even though Gawaine and I were very close friends, he was not one of us because, as great and powerful as he was, he was no match for any of us.

There was an unspoken agreement that none of us would ever fight either of the other two, since there was no way that any of us would ever yield or leave the field a beaten man. That agreement held, except for one instance, when Tristan and I did not recognize each other.

Lamorak was a crazy man in battle who sought out opportunities to fight against crowds of knights. Tournaments made him deliriously happy and, since I would not participate, he always came away with piles of armor and weapons and many horses as the spoils of war. It is a testament to the stupidity of most knights, that they dared to face him in jousts or melees. Perhaps their overwhelming desire to kill him overcame any modicum of common sense.

There was particularly bad blood between Lamorak and the sons of King Lot. After Lot died, Lamorak began a liaison with Queen Morgause, which may have started before the old king was dead. I have already mentioned how different Gareth, the youngest son, was in temperament and appearance from his brothers. His size, strength and friendly demeanor gave promise of him being a knight of enormous honor and prowess unmatchable by even Gawaine.

Unfortunately, I agreed with the gossip that it seemed unlikely that Gareth was the fruit of the old man Lot's loins.

Lamorak was killed when Gawaine, his brothers and several other knights caught him in an ambush and Mordaunt came up from behind and stabbed him with a knife. I was both angry and miserable when I heard about his death and the lowly, dishonorable act that caused it. Lamorak was worth more than all of them put together but, as expected, Arthur exonerated his nephews from any wrongdoing and I had no choice but to swallow my hatred of them and move on with my life. But, with Lamorak's murder, something else died, and that was the respect and affection that I had for Gawain. After all, the others could not have handled Lamorak without Gawain's help.

Deep in my heart I believed that some day, somehow, I would kill all of Lot's sons. The world, and the brotherhood of knights, would be better off without them.

Although he had not yet come to Arthur's court, Sir Tristan of Liones, at the age of sixteen, was already well known and honored. Everyone had heard how he freed Cornwall from paying tribute to Ireland by defeating Sir Morhaus, an experienced and deadly knight. We had, also, heard of his great service to his uncle, King Mark of Cornwall, by bringing Iseult from Ireland to be his bride.

Mark was not a king of great reputation, and there was no memory among any of Arthur's knights of him entering the lists of any tournament. Some believed that he had gained the throne through guile and opportunity rather than by right of birth or force of arms.

Unfortunately, Tristan had chosen Mark, instead of his own royal father, to make him a knight, and he was, therefore, bound by fealty and vassalage to do Mark's bidding. It was the height of knightly loyalty that caused Tristan to give up Iseult, who loved him with a passion and devotion equal to his own.

The first time I met Tristan, he was coming to Londinium and I was leaving. We encountered each other at a place where, many years earlier, the brothers Balin and Balan had, unknowingly, fought each other to the death. They were buried beside each other, and on their tomb was written a prophecy, supposedly made by Merlin, that the two greatest knights in the world would someday fight each other on that spot. It was a strange repetition of the past encounter between the tragic brothers. I carried a shield without markings and his shield was unknown to me. It felt to me as if our meeting had been fated, and it must have felt the same to Tristan.

It was the most magnificent battle I have ever fought. Neither one of us could stay in the saddle. We fought on foot for almost two hours, crashing into each other with our shields, trying to knock each other off balance, yet avoiding each other's sword as much as possible. Tristan had the advantage of youth, but I had the advantage of experience.

Finally, I could continue no longer and I held up my hand.

"Sir knight," I said, "you are the strongest and best knight I have ever met. If you give me leave, I will fight no more. But I must know who you are so that I may do you proper honor and thanks."

"Sir," he answered, "I am reluctant to tell you my name, since I am a knight of Cornwall, and I have met other knights from this country who have belittled me for it."

"I regret that greatly and I will ask no more. I will tell you my name if you ask."

"Well, then," he said, "what is your name?"

"Sir knight, I am called Lancelot of the Lake."

"Alas, alas," he cried, "I am cursed that I ever raised my hand against you. You are the man in the whole world that I love and honor the most."

"Fair knight," I said in astonishment, "I beg you, tell me your name."

"Truly, my name is Tristan of Liones."

"Oh, what terrible thing have I done?" I cried.

I kneeled down and yielded my sword to Tristan. And he kneeled before me and yielded his sword as well. Then our squires disarmed us, and we sat and embraced each other with great affection and respect and kissed each other in eternal friendship.

I returned to Londinium with Tristan, since I did not want to be parted from him, and I was anxious to present him to Arthur and Guinevere and see him welcomed in Arthur's court.

For months Tristan and I enjoyed each other's company, until word came from Cornwall that King Mark required his nephew's lance and sword to resolve a local conflict. There was no point in my urging him not to go, since his oath of loyalty was as strong as my own. Nevertheless, I watched him leave with great concern and trepidation. His love for Iseult, her love for him and a king without honor was a witch's brew of troubles.

A few months later, Tristan returned to Londinium with Iseult. Mark's jealousy had led him to attempt Tristan's murder and Iseult's imprisonment. They had escaped, but his concern for his love's safety had led him back to Arthur's court. He would have no more to fear. On a bright, sunny morning, the three of us, followed by fifty knights, rode out of Londinium and onward to Joyous Garde, where the two lovers could live in peace and tranquility with pages and squires and ladies and attendants and everything else they needed to live happily.

Then, one dark, terrible day, Tristan was called to see Arthur.

King Mark had demanded that Arthur force the return of Tristan and Iseult. When I heard of it, I went to Arthur and insisted that he ignore Mark. I warned him that Mark would find some way to kill Tristan and that the murder would be on his hands. I yelled, cursed, and threatened, but Arthur would have no part of it. I begged Tristan to stay in Joyous Garde, and swore to him that I would kill Arthur and all of his court for love of him and that he could stay there forever.

But, Tristan would not give me what I yearned for. Without Arthur's approval he could not stay.

I thought it was the worst day of my life when I saw Tristan ride away. I knew that I would never see him again. All of my anger was gone, replaced by a feeling of doom, not only for Tristan and Iseult, but for all of us.

I was sitting on an open window ledge looking down on the street below, crowded with people of all sorts scurrying about their daily business. As usual, the peat smoke was thick, the street stank of human and swine waste. I was not happy and thought of many places I would rather be. I would be gone, if I did not have a current obligation to Arthur.

There was a knock on the door and, at my response, one of Arthur's pages entered.

"My lord," he said, "the King wishes you to attend him immediately."

I rose from my perch and told the lad to lead on. There was nothing unusual in this summons and I did not belt on my sword.

It was a short walk from my lodging near the palace to Arthur's villa, and the page directed me to a large room where Arthur held audiences for foreign officials. A quick look around put me on my guard immediately. This was no routine summons.

Arthur sat on the raised dais with Gawain standing at his left and Agravaine and Gaheras standing behind their brother. All three wore sheathed swords.

Guinevere sat to the right of her husband, but slightly apart from him. Her hands gripped the carved ends of the armrests so tightly that her fingertips and knuckles were white. Her eyes, which were red from crying stared at me without blinking.

As I walked unsteadily toward the King, Lionel and Bors moved to either side of me and grasped my arms. Their support gave me some confidence that I was not to be murdered on the spot, but I quickly noticed that they were not armed and that dampened my confidence somewhat.

The King spoke first.

"Sir Lancelot, am I your liege lord to whom you have sworn fealty?"

"Yes, my Lord."

"Have you sworn to obey me in all things?"

"Yes, my lord, but only in all things that are honorable. On pain of death, I will refuse to bring dishonor on myself. What is more, honor and dishonor are mine alone to decide. There is no one in this world who has the power over me to require me to act dishonorably."

"That is well said, sir knight, and it would do you well to keep your vow before you as I tell you what I must."

I braced myself for the most terrible news I would ever hear.

"Sir Lancelot, it grieves me to tell you that Sir Tristan has been killed by King Mark."

I heard the words and then I heard nothing further except a loud roaring in my ears. My head felt as if it would burst. Then I felt the strength in every part of my body, as I tensed with a great angry rage. I bent my knees. I was going to leap on Arthur and tear his throat out. Gawain and his brothers were drawing their swords, but they were moving so slowly, they could not stop me.

As I surged forward, Lionel threw his arm around my neck and tried to drag me backwards. Bors ducked under my arms and shoved his shoulder into my waist, trying to do the same. I dragged them both to the foot of Arthur's chair. His eyes were wide with fright and I heard him scream, "Gawain, Gawain, stop him!"

Gawain did not move but Guinevere did. She stepped between us and, in spite of my roars, she whispered, "Stop, Lancelot. For love of me, please stop."

I do not remember hearing her above the noise, but I could read every word on her lips.

I stopped. My head throbbed and my body shook. I looked at Arthur, and I hoped that he could read the hatred I had for him on my face.

"I warned you. You are guilty of this crime," I growled.

I heard a gasp, as no one had ever spoken to the King in that tone of voice and without a respectful salutation.

"Lancelot, remember your vow. I order you to not seek vengeance ...."

Before he could finish, I interrupted with all the sneering sarcasm I could muster.

"Fear not, Sir King, I will not go to Cornwall, but if ever I lay my hands upon him in any other country, I will kill your Kingly friend in the most painful way I can devise. And, you, Sir King, need not fear me. Your punishment for this evil deed will come at the hands of another."

With those hateful words, I shook off my cousins and stormed out of the room and into the stink-filled streets of Londinium, which now smelled fresher and cleaner than Arthur's rooms.

Cornwall was not part of Arthur's domain. There was no vassalage between Arthur's Britain and Mark's Cornwall. Arthur had every right to deny Mark's demand for Tristan's return without risk of committing a violation of honor. War over this matter was out of the question, as Britain's size and strength was many times that of Cornwall. No, his decision was cold-hearted and intended to gain favor with a foreign king and gain any profit or riches that favor might bring with it.

What a terrible thing Niniane had done to me. She had bound me to Arthur. If King Gradlon had made me a knight, I would be vassal to an honorable king. Oh, to be a free man. I wish that one of us would die. I would be free either way.

I decided then and there that I would leave Londinium, whether Arthur needed me or not. Let him do without me for a while, then he might think carefully before he once again betrays someone I love.

Chapter 14

Springtime is the time for war.

An army cannot be moved for weeks or months across the country without supplies and especially without food and fresh water. If supplies cannot be transported by river craft, it must be carried by horse-drawn wagons. In winter the roads are hardly passable by heavy wagons. Wild game is scarce, and there is little or no food available for the taking at farms and settlements. So, springtime is the time for war because the weather is more settled and food is easier to find. Summer crops will have already been planted, so knights, free men and serfs, who work the land, can be drafted to fight, until they must return to their lands to harvest their crops in late autumn.

It was late March when messengers started arriving at Arthur's court to tell the King of a growing presence of Jutes arriving by boat at the mouth of the River Medford in eastern Kent. By April, Arthur's scouts reported that the number of Jutes had grown into the thousands and that they had begun to lay waste to the country in search of food, forage for their horses and weapons that the local British might have. Allowing the Jutes to gain a foothold and start building defensible settlements was unacceptable. There was no doubt that Arthur would have to raise an army and drive them out of Kent and back to where they came.

Arthur's war leaders were either in Londinium or at their own manors near the town. He sent messengers to them all, instructing them to meet with him as a war council. These men were Arthur's surviving allies and councilors from the early days of the civil wars and the battles against the Saxons. I was allowed to witness the meetings, but I was not allowed to speak or offer an opinion on a battle plan or strategy. Nevertheless, it was a useful experience to observe the heated give and take, and I gained a measure of respect for how Arthur maintained peace among strong-willed men who opposed each other. In the end, it was Arthur who decided how to proceed, and it was he who enforced acceptance and unity among the councilors.

Arthur was indeed a rich prince, as he was able to maintain one hundred knights as his personal guard. He ordered them to ride far and wide with all possible speed to summon his vassals and liegemen to war. Within days, a gathering started of kings, barons and other nobles with their sworn levy of mounted and armored knights, foot-soldiers and archers. By three weeks, Arthur had his army fully encamped on the outskirts of Londinium.

In general, the plan was for our foot soldiers to break open enemy infantry formations. Then our mounted knights would move to the forefront and begin slaying the infantrymen. The knights would cause further breakage in the enemy lines and wreak havoc amongst the infantrymen, as it is much easier to kill a man from the top of a horse than to stand on the ground and face a destrier carrying an armed knight.

It was also vital that we catch the enemy in an open, flat plain because our knights would be at a disadvantage on rough and hilly ground where we could not mount an overpowering charge. Each knight, such as myself, was to be armed with chainmail, an iron helmet and breastplate and carry a shield and lance as well as a sword and any other preferred weapons. We would charge into battle leading our similarly mounted and armed squires and liegemen.

We could expect the enemy infantry to use long spears, javelins, maces, gisarmes and axes and protect themselves with circular shields. Their bowman would fire at close range. In fighting against knights, their intent was to bring down our horses, so that they could swarm all over us and kill or capture us for ransom.

From scouts and spies Arthur learned that the Jutes had gathered their forces on the north side of the River Medford near the town of Strood. On the south side of the river were three small towns: Brom, Gillford and Chatswold, which were on the outskirts of a large, open plain where the battle would be fought.

A large and sturdy bridge crossed the river at Strood. The Jutes built two more bridges and fortified the crossings with stockades. The nearby hill forts were repaired, where necessary, and reinforced. For several days, the Jutes crossed the river and set up temporary camps. First came the foot-soldiers, archers and other infantry men. Then wagons bearing armor, weapons and supplies came across, and finally the knights, their squires and horses crossed.

Our army began a long, strung out march that was planned to take three days to reach Chatswold. When our leading infantry reached the three towns, the Jute infantry engaged our warriors in skirmishes. Losses were light in these early battles, but it did not take much for the towns to be heavily damaged. It took five more days after the first contacts, for all of Arthur's army to form up and prepare for all out war. During that time, the entire Jute force had crossed the river and made their preparations.

Arthur's army was divided into units led by experienced war leaders. A knight, who was especially deserving of the honor, rode beside the war leader throughout the battle, carrying aloft a flag showing the leader's coat of arms. Fifty to one hundred knights and squires, who owed fealty to the leader, and as many as two hundred and fifty foot soldiers and archers followed and fought under that flag. The war leader knew the battle plan. He knew where to attack, when to advance and when to carry out a tactical retreat. The exception was what Arthur called shock troops. Certain knights were chosen to roam the battlefield with a small cadre of their own liegemen and squires and bolster those lines that were in danger of falling back. Gawain and his brothers were one such force. My cousins, Lionel and Bors, and I, along with our squires were another shock troop. Sir Cai and Sir Bedevere, among others, also led such forces.

On a dark Tuesday morning our British army heard a Christian mass by the Bishop of Canterbury and redeployed according to the flags of their lords, so that by the time the sun was up, the two armies were formed in opposing lines. The forces under King Urien guarded our left flank. King Carvados and his people protected our right flank. Our main force was led, of course, by the King. The Jutes were comprised of foot soldiers and archers supported by mounted knights who were formidable and dangerous but not mounted or armed nearly as well as Arthur's knights. Their real advantage was in their numbers, as there were easily two of theirs opposed to one of ours.

I had never been in a battle such as this, and as I sat in the saddle waiting and looking over the masses of men and animals, I thought that hundreds of thousands of men would be killing each other. But, older and more experienced heads told me later that the number was about twenty thousand and that the dead would number no more than half. Regardless of the estimates, the plain would be completely covered by the corpses of men and horses when the battle was over.

At the signal of a bugle blast, King Urien attacked the enemy's right flank and King Carvados attacked their left side. The Jutish knights met the attacks, and the fighting, once started, ebbed and flowed, forward and back as one side or the other gained or lost ground. The opposing sides were so intermingled and pressed so closely that it was impossible to use spears or swords and the men fought with axes and clubs. Arrows rained down on friend and foe alike, as they were unable to cover themselves with shields. The plain was soon littered with bodies. The screams of horses and men rose above the din of clashing weapons and roars of fear or victory. Foot soldiers on both sides were exhausted. The grassy plain became matted with pools of blood. There were piles of dead and dying in every direction, and the living thought nothing of climbing over dead bodies to fight or retreat.

After one hour, I could see from a low hilltop that King Urien's forces were beginning to waver and then retreat. Lionel, Bors and I and our squires spurred our horses toward Urien's flag.

I had already decided that this was no time for jousting with a lance. Knights and foot soldiers were massed and fighting in a great melee without any rules of organized combat. It was kill or be killed, and staying alive meant killing or maiming anyone, knight or varlet, who meant to do me harm. I was not riding Fer de Blanc for fear of losing him, but the destrier I rode was nearly as strong and brave. I crashed him into the Jutish line swinging my sword first to the left and then to the right. I knew that Lionel and Bors were near, but all I could see were arms and legs to be slashed, shields to be split and heads, with or without helmets, to be separated from their bodies.

It was not long before I sensed that the Jutish line was moving away from me and none of their men were within reach. I spurred the destrier forward and the enemy line kept retreating, as if I were pushing on a loose thread with my finger. The noise was deafening. Cries of despair and encouragement all blended into a roar so loud that I could not hear anything, except the pounding in my own head. But, finally, I heard, behind me, the roar of Urien's troops as they realized that they could follow me to victory. They surged past me, their flags waving, as the Jutes fell into full retreat. But the battle was by no means over.

King Carvados had been holding out on our right flank. But, the situation changed suddenly for the worse when the Jutes sent more than one thousand of their strongest mounted knights, whom they had held in reserve, against the King. This was the main strength of the Jute army. Gawain and his brothers saw the danger and rode swiftly to the rescue, but even Gawain's fierce prowess was not enough to stop the slaughter of Carvados' people.

Arthur also saw the Jute strategy, and at his signal, the reserve of the British forces poured into what was now the main battle on the right flank. After several hours of massed battle, the Jutish knights began to get the upper hand and a number of British flags disappeared. And then I saw the Jutish king, at the head of more than one hundred mounted knights, charging swiftly and directly at King Arthur. The hair on the back of my neck stood up and I shuddered. If

Arthur were killed or taken prisoner that would be the end of Britain.

"To Arthur," I roared, and spurred my destrier viciously. I hoped that Lionel and Bors were with me, but I did not really care. All I wanted to do was to reach the King.

It seemed as if I was hardly moving, yet bodies and flags and banners flew past me. I sensed the fighting rage on all around me, yet I saw nothing but Arthur's flag. The destrier was galloping at full speed and then, without hesitation or warning, we crashed headlong into the rear of the massed Jutish knights surrounding Arthur's position.

I do not remember anything of what happened next.

I must have been asleep because when I opened my eyes my cousins, Arthur, Gawain and dozens of other knights were standing around me, watching me intently and whispering among themselves. I realized that I was lying on the ground almost naked and that Loegaire was washing blood, which was not mine, off my face. It seemed strange to me that so many brave and famous knights would be watching me sleep. Then Arthur came towards me. He reached down and grasped my hand. Without a word, he squeezed it and smiled at me. Then he stood up, turned and walked away followed by all of the others except Lionel, Bors and, of course, faithful Loegaire.

Yvain, who was with Arthur during that last Jutish charge against the King, told me that wherever I went in that melee the Jutes melted away like winter snow dropped on a hearth before a burning fireplace. Gawain told me that I was like a river of death around the King, and that everyone who tried to get near him drowned in his own blood.

The Jutes were annihilated. Those who were not killed or maimed fled to the river in an effort to escape. But, our forces had taken control of the three bridges, and the Jutes had no choice but to swim. Many drowned, pulled down by the weight of their armor, which they valued more than their own lives. Others drowned from exhaustion or loss of blood. Very few achieved the bank on the north side of the river where Arthur's men were waiting to take them prisoner.

We had lost many brave knights and thousands of men who were husbands and fathers and brothers who had been called from their fields and shops to fight for their King and defend land that was not their own. But, this is what was needed if we were to have a united Britain.

Scavengers were already stripping the dead bodies of everything of value. Pavilions were set up so that surgeons could do what they could to save the wounded, and burial details were digging trenches for the human corpses. The King was preparing to return to Winchester for a proper victory celebration. Lionel and Bors wanted to accompany the King. But, the sight of the carnage wearied me. Nothing I had done had brought me a shred of honor. I had maimed and killed like a wild beast, and victory gave me no comfort. I hated war and never wanted to fight in one again. But, I knew that I could not escape the world and I would go to war again. For now, I just wanted to be alone with my thoughts and my sadness. My ever-faithful squires followed me as I turned my back to that field of death and rode slowly towards the forest.

Chapter 15

We rode aimlessly for several days, while I struggled to clear myself of the dark mood I was in. So much blood had been spilled. It was like a slaughterhouse, and I wanted to forget all of it.

On the third day, we came upon a very pleasant and prosperous looking town surrounding a small but elegant castle with a tall tower. As we rode at a slow pace through the town, people gathered around us shouting my name, cheering and welcoming me. It was a nice surprise to see that I was favorably well known in such an out-of-the-way place. I enjoyed the adulation, and it definitely helped to brighten my mood.

A well dressed page, no more than nine or ten years old, came out of the crowd of townspeople and addressed me.

"My lord, Sir Lancelot, my master, King Pelles of Corbin begs you to accept his hospitality at his castle. He wishes to give you and your squires rest and comfort and comfortable lodging for the night or as long as you will stay. If you will do so, please come with me."

I nodded my agreement and the boy turned and walked briskly in the direction of the castle gate. We followed and left the crowd behind us still chanting my name, waving and hip-hooraying.

We were not far from the castle, and after passing through the gate, we entered the courtyard where a number of pages and squires awaited us. They relieved us of our horses and arms and bustled around us doing what they could to make us feel at ease. Even Cael, Loegaire and Brandon were made exceedingly welcome as they were led away to where they would be fed, made comfortable and have their needs seen to.

The page asked me to follow him again, and we passed from the courtyard into a large formal garden filled with shade trees, shrubs that had been trimmed and shaped and a plethora of flowers, whose scents were almost overpowering. There were also a number of smallish trees that I thought might be fruit bearing, but I did not recognize what they were.

King Pelles was waiting for me. He was a tall, handsome, well-built man of perhaps sixty years with white hair and a white beard. He had clear blue eyes and a warm and friendly countenance. His smile showed good teeth for a man his age.

He welcomed me and we shook hands. He took my arm and led me through the garden pointing out and naming interesting plants along the way. In answer to my question, he confirmed that the small trees were indeed fruit bearing and that I was unfamiliar with them because they had been brought from a faraway land called Judea.

We continued to walk and talk until we entered the main hall of the castle and passed into a room that looked out into the garden. It was one of the most comfortable and inviting rooms I have ever been in. Rugs from the Levant, with intricate patterns and vibrant colors, covered the stone floor, and tapestries depicting Greek and Roman gods and goddesses hung on the walls. The room was still bright with light that came through a large window, and torches were placed in sconces on the walls to be lit when it became dark. There was an opening in the ceiling for smoke from the torches to escape. There were no tables or chairs in the room, but large pillows, covered in fantastic designs, were strewn all about on the rugs, and there were two small benches, no more than two handbreadths high, placed side by side.

The King sat down on the floor and adjusted the pillows, so that he was propped into a reclining position. He invited me to sit as well, and I smiled as I imagined myself as a reclining eastern potentate. When I was settled, he clapped his hands and several pages entered carrying salvers of food and drink, which they placed on the benches. He noticed my hesitancy, but encouraged me to be adventurous and brave and try the foods that were unlike anything I had ever seen or tasted.

There were small cubes of roasted meat pierced by a tiny wooden spear that were so savory and tender that I did not want to stop eating them. There were pastries stuffed with beef and a flat bread that we dipped into oil made from olives. There was a cooked grain called rice, beans, mashed and whole, and vegetables that I had never heard of. They were all cooked with savory sauces made with spices that made my mouth a place of wonder and discovery, and made my tongue tingle and burn in a most pleasant manner. There were fruits that had come from the King's trees that were sweet beyond comprehension. And then there was a wine that was so sweet that it seemed to make me happier than I had ever been.

All through the meal, the pages came and went, bringing new dishes and replenishing the wine. The King and I talked about many things, and he was interested to hear about Arthur and Merlin and many knights that he had known in the past. He told me about his travels to Greece and Rome, to the land that was called Carthage and is across the great sea, and especially about Judea.

We talked and ate and drank until it was just before night. And then I closed my eyes and fell asleep.

I thought that I was dreaming. It was like a dream I had so often when I was younger, and then woke with my thighs covered in a sticky wetness. But, this time, it was not a dream. I opened my eyes and tried to move, but I could not move except to turn my head. I was naked, lying on a bed. Someone came towards me and leaned over me. She started kissing me. She was naked and her breasts grazed my chest. She kept kissing me and then reached down and started stroking my thighs and then my privates. My head pounded and my breath came in short gasps. I started to shake, and I felt like I would break into pieces and fly apart.

She climbed on top of me, her legs spread to either side. I was engulfed in something wet and warm, and she began to move up and down on me. I felt like the life was draining out of me and pouring into my groin. I tried to scream, but all I heard coming from me was a howl like that of a wild animal. Then my hips rose and fell with her, and I burst like I had never done before.

She got off me, covered herself and laid down beside me. I saw from the corner of my eye that she was crying.

I went to sleep.

The next morning the first thing I felt, even before opening my eyes, was a pain in my head, the worst pain I have ever felt. The room was light, and when I opened my eyes, it felt as if knife blades had been thrust into them. I covered my eyes with my hands to ease the pain, but I had to see where I was. I spread my fingers a bit and looked around.

She was there. It had not been a dream. She was a demon, and she had defiled me. She was asleep, and I kicked at her with my bare feet. She flew out of the bed and landed on the floor half way across the room. She was fully awake now, and I saw the terror in her eyes as she tried to scurry away from me.

I leaped out of bed and looked quickly for a weapon, but there was none. No matter. I dove for the demon, determined to strangle it, even if it cost me my life. But, just as I had my hands around its neck, I heard King Pelles cry out.

"Sir Lancelot, my lord. Please stop or you will kill my daughter, Aileen, and your unborn son."

"I only half heard him, but what he said was enough to stop me.

"You monster," I growled, "what kind of evil creature are you? You shall die right here by my hand."

She was sobbing with tears streaming from her eyes. "Fair, courteous knight, I beg you to have mercy upon me."

"Sir," she said trembling, "I am Aileen, the daughter of King Pelles. You are blameless of any sin. What you have done was done through prophecy and enchantment. As you are the greatest knight of the world, do not kill me. I have in my womb your only son, who shall be the noblest knight of the world. He shall sit in the Siege Perilous and he shall find our Lord's holy cup and take it to Heaven."

I released my grip on her throat and rolled off her and onto the floor. I was shaking with anger and the urge to kill both father and daughter was almost overwhelming. But, I am not an ignorant brute who kills without thinking. Besides, this was a maiden, and not a demon, I had lain with and by my vows, I could not harm her.

"Take this evil person from my sight and get away from me yourself. I wish not to do you harm for the sin that I have committed. Get out, both of you."

Ah, this was indeed the most evil day of my life. I had refused every temptation for love of Guinevere. Now I had broken the vows of faithfulness and chastity I had made to the Queen. I was a miscreant without honor. I would die, without honor, with a knife in my back or hung from a tree. The Queen would hear of my sin. She would damn me as a whoremonger. I would be shunned by every honorable knight and I would have to leave Arthur's court in shame and disgrace.

My anger and disgust with myself was beyond measure. I had allowed myself to be seduced. I had indulged myself in the pleasures of food and wine. I had ignored the disciplines of moderation and caution. I was responsible for my sin.

By mid-morning I had calmed down somewhat, and I was anxious to leave that unholy place. I opened the door to call for my squires, but King Pelles was standing there.

Before I could say a word, he held up his hand to stop me.

"Sir Lancelot," he said, "you have reason to hate me and wish to kill me and my daughter, but you must hear what I have to say."

I did not respond, so he started.

"Sir knight, you know the story of the Grail Knight. He must be the purest knight in the world in order to find Christ's cup and deliver it to Heaven. Your Lady Niniane raised you to be the Grail Knight. But, you are not that knight because you are not innocent. You have lain with women and your love and passion for Queen Guinevere mean that you are not an innocent knight. Still, the blood of Joseph of Arimathea flows through you, as it did through your father King Ban of Benoic. Joseph's blood will, therefore, flow through your son as well.

"My daughter, Aileen, was chosen to be the vessel of the true Grail Knight. Because of your great love and loyalty toward the Queen, you would not have consented to lie with her. The wine you drank last night rendered you unable to resist and, therefore, the sin is not yours.

"The wine you drank came from grapes grown in a special, blessed vineyard in Judea. The wine our Lord drank, before he was slain, was made from grapes grown in that same vineyard.

"Sir knight, do not despair, I beg you. You are not cursed. You are blessed. Do not seek to understand. The powers that shape the world are too great for our comprehension."

I did not want to hear any more of that talk. I needed time and solitude to think about what had happened and what I should do next. I pushed the King aside and went to find my squires. As quickly as we could, we dressed and packed and rode out of the castle and away from that accursed town.

As we rode undisturbed through the forest, once more, one thought kept coming back to me. Both Pelles and his daughter said that she was carrying my unborn child. How did they know that? Oh, well, to Hades with the two of them. I was tired of all the magic and prophecies and gods and holy cups. No cup would save Britain from its enemies. Britain needed only a king like Arthur, and lances and swords and knights like me in order to be free.

As we rode further away from Corbenic, all of my anger was replaced by an equal measure of dread. Pelles was no aggrieved father who would keep his daughter's shame a secret from the world. To the contrary, he was beyond joy at the event, and he would noise it everywhere.

There was no place for me to hide from this terrible sin I had committed. I rode away, aimlessly, with my squires, who knew all that had happened and were now as miserable as I was.

The next few months are still a blur to me. All that I remember about that time is the wandering and the fighting. I challenged every knight who had the great misfortune to cross my path. Whether he was a knight of Arthur's court or not, I beat him into submission. I went after bands of thieves and cutthroats. I threw myself into every dangerous encounter with the morbid hope that someone would kill me and end my shame. But that did not happen. The worst I could accomplish was a scratch or bruise.

In the meantime, the first news of my liaison with Aileen spread to Arthur's court. Then, after a few months, it became known that Aileen was pregnant with my child. From the moment of hearing the first rumor, Guinevere's anger was beyond measure. There was no doubt in her mind that I had committed the unforgiveable sin, and the thought that I had betrayed my promise to her and loved another woman made her furious. She scorned, rebuked and reviled me at every opportunity and would not listen to Bors or Lionel when they tried to explain how a dishonorable father, who was determined to have Lancelot's son, had ensnared me.

As winter approached, I accepted the inevitable. The squires had suffered enough for their loyalty to me. It was time to take them home to Londinium. I cheered myself a bit by imagining that I had nothing to be afraid of and that no one in the court would know what happened.

We rode into Londinium on a dark and rainy day and headed directly to my lodgings in Arthur's palace. In spite of the miserable weather, there were enough people out and about to see our approach and to recognize me.

My apprehension immediately grew as I noticed the whispering and the sly looks directed at me. I dug my spurs into the palfrey, and he jumped into a fast trot that carried me quickly into the courtyard where the pages, hearing the hoof beats, came running to take the horses and our gear.

Without a word in response to the welcomes from my household, I almost ran to my rooms, where I was attended to, and changed into comfortable clothing. I went to bed and there I stayed, saying nothing to anyone, not allowing visitors (including my cousins), and letting everyone cater to me and provide for me, as they saw fit and proper. But no comfort or care could assuage my feelings of forthcoming doom and disaster.

My protective isolation lasted only three precious days. Then a page came from Arthur himself requesting my immediate attendance. The summons fell on me like an axe. I could not breathe and my chest pounded as if something inside wanted to come out. More than ever, I wanted to die.

As I approached Arthur's throne room, I could hear the loud chatter of a large crowd of people waiting for me. When I crossed under the archway into the room, the crowd turned toward me and fell completely silent. I hesitated for a moment, took a deep breath and walked forward towards the King on legs that were much too shaky for the greatest knight in the entire realm.

Arthur was staring right at me with a big smile on his face that reflected his glee at my misery and discomfort. A quick glance to Arthur's right was enough to confirm my worst fears. Guinevere looked at me with venomous hate in her eyes.

I looked around the hall for someone to rescue me. Lionel and Bors were there as was Percival, but their frowns were not encouraging. There were many others who were there to support me: knights of Brittany, knights who were my liegemen by birth and by right of combat, men who were proud to have fought against me and lived to swear allegiance to me.

Then there were those who could hardly withhold their joy at my troubles. Agravaine and Gaheris hated me for untold reasons, as did Mordaunt and the knights who supported the ambitions of those three miscreants.

"Sir Lancelot," Arthur boomed for all to hear, "you are most welcome back. You have been away from us far too long, and we have missed your happy presence. But then, you must have many adventures to tell us about."

"Yes, my Lord, I have fought many battles since last spring and I have brought the King's peace and justice to many lands during my wandering."

Then a cold, harsh voice cut through the meaningless banter.

"Sir Lancelot," the Queen snarled, "we are all interested in your magnificent victories, but before you regale us with tales of your battles and heroism, please tell us how you managed to beget a brat on that whore daughter of King Pelles.

"False traitor knight that you are," she screamed, "leave my court, forever. Get out and never dare to come into my sight again."

I do not remember what happened next, or what happened for some time after that. All that I can tell you is what my squires related to me, after I regained my senses, and what Lionel, Bors and Percival told me long ago.

Apparently, I immediately turned my back on the King and Queen and walked out of the throne room and out of the castle. My friends assumed that I would return to my lodging, prepare myself and leave Londinium for Joyous Garde. But, instead, after leaving the castle, I walked and walked for hours, until the rain turned to snow and by nightfall I had disappeared.

The rest of this part of my life is very hard for me to relate. But though I have no recollections of my own, the truth of it has been attested to, by the knights and ladies who cared for and protected me, and by my family, squires and friends, who searched for me through the winter and into the spring of the following year.

Bors, Lionel and Percival had witnessed my public humiliation and how I reacted. As soon as I was gone, Guinevere went to her rooms. My cousins were stunned by the Queen's vicious tirade, and feared that the worst was yet to come. They followed her and when they were alone with her, they warned that she would be to blame for whatever I might do. They also warned the Queen that she had caused a breach between the two of us that might never be completely healed, and that although loyalty and honor required me to remain her champion, I would never again love her as I once did.

The Queen reacted to these warnings with scorn and derision and continued to defile me with accusations of infidelity, perfidy and loathful licentiousness. Distraught over the terrible turn of events, my cousins left her and made their way to my lodgings. Cael, who seemed to know about everything happening to me almost as soon as it happened, was waiting anxiously for my return. When Bors and the others appeared, he realized that something was wrong and quickly informed the knights of my absence.

All of the squires and pages were immediately sent out to look for me. Lionel, Bors and Percival took horses from my stables and joined the search riding bareback.

Starting from Arthur's lodgings, the searchers went in every direction, but the snow had become heavier and the wind stronger. Any footprints that I might have made earlier were covered or blown away. By nightfall, the search was abandoned, and Bors and the others went to the Queen to tell her that I could not be found.

My disappearance in such terrible weather, without anyone to look out for me and without warm clothes, a horse and armor, or food or gold, finally began to convince Guinevere of the seriousness of the situation and the destructive effect her public debasement had had on me.

"Alas," she said, "What have I done? I was wrong to accuse him of being false to me. I am the most accursed and stupid woman in the world. I know that I have lost him for ever." Then she cried as though she thought that I was dead.

"Lady," said Bors, "it is we who are accursed. It is our sin that Lancelot and his kin ever came to your court. You have destroyed the best knight of our blood. He was our leader and our help in all things, and I dare say we will never see another knight of his nobility and courtesy, and with his beauty and his gentleness."

When the Queen heard what Bors said, she fell to the ground in a dead faint. Bors picked her up, sat her on a chair and fanned her. When she came to her senses, she slipped to the floor, kneeled before the three knights, held up both her hands, and begged them to go after me and find me. Then she gave them all the gold and silver she had and told them to spare no expense in their search.

All through that miserable winter Bors, Percival, and Lionel went their separate ways and rode from country to country, in forests, wildernesses and in wastelands. They stopped and spoke to all types of men to ask and listen for news of a man resembling me. They suffered greatly in their quest and often went without food and lodging. But, for all their effort, they heard no word of me and reluctantly returned to Londinium in failure.

I had walked out of the assembly hall through the courtyard and gardens and out toward the river. I passed the quays until I reached the bridge and then crossed the river to the south bank. I passed through a small cemetery and plunged into the marshland at the bend of the river. I must have been all wet and near freezing by the time I left the marsh and entered the woods.

I was dressed only in a light linen tunic and linen trousers. On my legs and feet were thin shoes and woolen leggings. I am sure that I would have soon died from exposure had it not been for my faithful squire, Loegaire.

The young man had followed me into the assembly hall and had seen and heard all that transpired. When I left the hall, he followed me, and when he realized that I was not returning to my lodging, he helped himself to a plug horse that was at hand and continued to follow me at a respectful distance. It was long after entering the woods that I collapsed. Loegaire rushed up to me and dragged me into a small copse, somewhat protecting me from the falling snow. He removed all of my wet clothing and wrapped me, first, in his woolen cape and then in a horse blanket. He sat me up but could not get me to speak or respond to him in any way other than to obey his instructions.

It was then that Loegaire made a fateful decision. He would not bring an insane Lancelot back to Arthur's court. He would hide me away until I regained my sanity or until some higher power, greater and wiser than he, told him to do otherwise. Loegaire was wise beyond his years. He was sure that if Lionel and Bors saw their cousin in his present condition, they would murder Guinevere on the spot. A terrible war would ensue, since there were many kings and knights who loved me or owed me fealty and hated Arthur and the sons of King Lot.

Loegaire knew of a woodsman's hut that he had found while adventuring in the forest as a young page. He picked me up in his arms, hoisted me across his shoulder and heaved me across the horse's back. Then, leading the horse by the bridle, he trudged off deeper into the forest.

The hut was built mostly underground and was well secluded and hidden from anyone without prior knowledge of its existence. After a few coins changed hands, the poor man, who lived there alone, agreed to provide us the shelter we needed so desperately. While the man took the horse, Loegaire carried me into the hut and laid me on the dirt floor beside a weak fire on the hearth. It was not long, though, before the fire was blazing, as Loegaire threw on every item made of wood that the man possessed.

The next morning, after feeding me as best he could, Loegaire instructed the woodsman, on pain of death, to watch over me and keep me safe until he returned from London.

At eighteen years of age and almost a knight, my squire was big and strong and with a double-edged sword, he appeared fearsome and awesome, when he chose. He put the fear of death and the hope for reward in the woodsman and rode the horse bareback towards Londinium, reasonably sure that I would be where he left me when he returned.

When Loegaire reached London and entered my lodging, no one was surprised, since all of the squires and pages came and went with the search parties still out looking for me.

Loegaire busied himself gathering the most necessary supplies for travel, and stuffed a pouch with gold and silver coins. Then he waited for Cael and Brendan.

When the two squires returned, they rushed to embrace their compatriot but were surprised to see him in my chambers. Loegaire quickly told them what had happened, what had happened to me, and what he had done.

It was then, on the spot, that the three of them hatched their plot to look after me while keeping the secret of my whereabouts and condition. They assembled all that was needed for winter travel and loaded packhorses with those supplies, as well as my armor and those weapons that could be hidden in the packs. Then the three young men, whom one day I would be honored to offer the accolade of knighthood, waited.

When night fell, the three mounted squires, leading my palfrey and two pack animals, rode out of the palace grounds, down to the river, across the bridge and headed south toward where I was hidden away.

Cael's father was Carodoc the King of Gwent in southeast Wales. The squires decided that because Cael's home was the furthest from London and his father was my devoted liegeman, they should take me there. Carodoc would hide me well and find me what help he could to cure my madness. He would also advise the squires on the wisest course.

Cael, Brendan and Loegaire were squires that any knight would be proud of. Each of them was big, strong, and well trained at arms. They had great courage, loyalty and devotion, and each of them would gladly give his life to save mine.

As the four of us traveled the smaller roads towards Gwent, we must have presented a valuable target for thieves with the quality of our mounts, the richness of the squire's armor and weapons and the heavily laden packhorses.

On the second day of our journey, we were attacked by a large band of thieves, some on foot and many others on horses and armored as knights. By prior agreement Cael held back, to protect me, while Brendan and Loegaire advanced to meet the attack with their swords.

The battle was hopelessly one-sided. In spite of their strength and prowess, the squires were greatly outnumbered and the footpads had attacked their horses, which received many wounds. Brendan and Loegaire were forced to retreat and surround me for my protection, but one of the false knights broke through and, with his sword raised, was about to strike Loegaire from behind.

I remember nothing. All that happened has been told to me by those who love me but, since they have been known to exaggerate my deeds, I cannot swear to the truth of any of it.

Nevertheless, they say that I caught the miscreant's arm, tore the sword from his hand and decapitated him with one blow. His brief shriek made everyone pause, and I went berserk, crashing my horse through the thieves and slashing at them left and right so that blood spurted everywhere.

Those left mounted or still standing ran from the field, but the ground was littered with dead and dying. With no one left to fight, I became calm as quickly as I had become enraged. Brandon took the reins of my horse, and the four of us rode away from the sight of all that carnage.

In a short while, we came to a stream where we all dismounted. Cael led me to the water, where he washed away the blood that had spattered me. I allowed him to wash me, but I would not release the sword, even when he tried to pry my fingers open. That is the way it was from then on. Awake or asleep, I would not give up the sword of a thief.

As we rode, day after day, the nature of my madness did not change. I did not speak, even to respond to questions. I did not nod or shake my head yes or no. I ate what was given to me, and obeyed the instructions of my squires without resistance or objection (except for relinquishing the sword). I did not appear to care for my comfort. Cold or hot, wet or dry meant nothing. I slept quietly, apparently without dreams.

We traveled at a moderate pace for many days without an incident of any sort. Then, one misty morning everything changed. We encountered a richly accoutered knight, who appeared well armed and mounted on a fine courser. As he approached, with his squires behind him, he raised his open hand toward us in a gesture of friendly greeting. No one expected my reaction.

I raised the sword and kicked my mount viciously into a gallop. The knight must have been surprised to see a large man, dressed only in linen, charging him like a madman with only a sword.

I was upon him before he could prepare himself. He had partially drawn his sword from its scabbard when I dropped my sword and leaped from my horse onto him. My weight forced him sideways, and he fell to the ground with me on top of him. He lost his breath, momentarily, but that was enough time for me to rip his sword from his hand. I raised the weapon and was about to cut the knight's throat, when Loegaire grabbed my arm with all the strength he had.

"No, Sir Lancelot, no," Loegaire screamed. "My lord, Lancelot, as you are a true knight, stop."

Loegaire swears that if I had wanted to kill that knight, he could not have stopped me. But what he lacked in overwhelming strength, he more than made up for in wisdom. Deeper than any sin I had committed with a woman, would have been the sin and dishonor of killing a helpless, innocent man. Loegaire's words had awakened and saved me. Here I was, Lancelot, crouched over a disarmed knight with a sword in my hand. I threw the blade aside, crawled off my victim and for the first time in my life, I cried.

Sir Bliant was a knight of Arthur's court and was well aware of what had transpired between the Queen and me. He knew that I had disappeared, but recognized me immediately when he first saw us. He was coming toward us in friendship and knightly brotherhood, when I attacked him without warning. Nevertheless, as he watched me sitting on the wet ground, with my head on my knees, shaking miserably, his kindness and concern overcame any anger or resentment he might have felt.

My sudden recollection of who I was did not extend to remembrance of what had transpired since I heard Guinevere's cruel denunciation. I struggled to make sense of where I was and what I was doing, but I quickly realized that was hopeless.

Brandon, Cael and Loegaire kneeled around me and started asking questions and interrupting each other like magpies. Finally, I held up my hand for silence.

"My friends, I know that I am Lancelot, but I do not remember anything since I was last in Londinium. I do not know where I am or what I have done or if I have brought shame or dishonor on my name in any way. I beg you to tell me all these things, but first I must know who this good knight is, and if I have done him any harm."

"My lord, Lancelot," the knight said as he knelt down next to my squires, "my name is Bliant, and I am a knight in Arthur's court. It has been more than one month since you left Londinium, and it is widely believed that you were lost and perished somewhere because of the bitter cold for which you were not dressed. Many knights and others have searched for you far and wide, and the court, especially the Queen, is distraught at having lost you."

At the mention of the Queen, I shivered, but I turned toward Brendan without a word.

"My lord," he said, "Loegaire followed you from the palace. When you could go no further, he arranged for your safety and brought us to you. You would not speak, and you did not know that you are Sir Lancelot. So, we believed that madness had overtaken you, and we would not bring you back to the King. We were taking you to Gwent and Cael's father, when we encountered Sir Bliant, who you were about to slay in your madness, but your reason returned.

"My lord, nothing has happened while you were in our care that besmirches your honor."

I looked at the three young men around me and could not speak, for lack of the words and calmness, of the gratitude I felt toward them for saving my life and my good name.

Sir Bliant was a knight of great generosity and hospitality. We were all taken to his castle, where we had comfortable lodgings, and were welcome to stay as long as we wished.

Over the next weeks, I spent most of every day in training with Brendan, Loegaire and Cael. I fought with them for hours on end, teaching them everything I had learned in so many battles. I made them practice with every weapon, until I was confident that they had reached their limits of strength and prowess.

Finally, I realized that I could do no more and that I was delaying the day that would give me both great happiness and an equal measure of sadness and regret.

For want of a better or warmer place, we gathered in the small Knight's Hall in Sir Bliant's palace. He and all of his knights, squires, pages and all of the ladies of the palace stood facing me.

As Brendan knelt before me, I tapped first one shoulder and then the next, with his own sword, and said "Sir Brandon, I dub thee knight." Then Sir Bliant and I knelt to tie on his spurs.

Loegaire knelt next and received the accolade from me in the same manner, except that Sir Brendan and I put on his spurs.

And last, Cael received the accolade and his spurs were tied on by Sir Loegaire and me.

I looked at the three new knights that I had made, and I felt more pride than I had ever felt in any battle. Though there were not many years between us, it seemed as if these were my sons that I had helped to grow into manhood. They were going into the world with full knowledge of the joys and struggles of knighthood. Their duties and actions as knights would always be shaped by their memory of Lancelot.

And then I knew what I would do for the rest of my life. I had a son about to be born. I had no father in my life, but my son would not be so deprived. I would go to him and help him to be the greatest knight in the world.

In a few days, Sir Brendan, Sir Loegaire and Sir Cael said their bitter-sweet goodbyes to each other and to me and went their separate ways. I said a grateful goodbye to Sir Bliant and set off toward Castle Corbin.

It was the first time in my life that I was alone.

When I returned to Castle Corbin and agreed to stay, King Pelles made me a gift of a large manor on a heavily treed island formed by two rivers that flowed around it. The manor had a villa, built in the Roman style, with baths and hot water. He offered me his knights, but I refused them. However, I accepted four young squires whom I trained for knighthood. The King hoped that Aileen and I would live as man and wife, but she had no interest in that. She spent her time praying, and I came to think of her as the one the priests call the Virgin Mother. Fortunately for me, all of her lady attendants were old enough to be Merlin's mother.

I called that place, surrounded by water, Joyous Isle, to remind me of my real home. I thought that when Galahad was of age I would give him Joyous Isle and Joyous Garde. Unlike me, he would not start out as a landless knight. I put no credence in it but if he truly was the Grail Knight, he would die in Niniane's quest and he would inherit nothing. In that case, everything I had would belong to the next king of Britain. But, I was sure that he would not die before me, at least not by carrying that cup to Heaven.

I made a vow to myself that my son would be well trained as a page and a squire. Then, if he wished to be a knight, I would perform the accolade and he would have my sword and spurs.

It was not long after settling in at Joyous Isle that I became miserably bored. There was practically nothing to do but watch the grass and my son grow. I had named him Galahad. That was my name and my grandfather's name before me. He was a sturdy little fellow and he crawled everywhere and got into all the mischief he was capable of. He would be walking soon and be an even greater handful for his nurse. He had my hair color and eyes and an attitude that left no doubt as to his parentage.

I wandered around with nothing important or exciting to do and I started to have all sorts of mad thoughts. I wondered if I should go back to Brittany to see the land where I was born and visit the graves of my father and mother. I thought it would be good to see King Gradlon again, if he was still alive.

I wondered if it was possible to reclaim Benoic for myself, and Ganis for Lionel and Bors. I had heard that King Claudas was dead and that Claudas II reigned over that country. The three of us could raise one thousand knights to fight against that usurper. We could swear fealty to King Gradlon, if he would raise an army to fight for us.

Then, out of the blue, I decided to return to Arthur's court. It was time to see old friends and for tournaments and feasts.

I had not seen Guinevere in a long while and things would be different between us. I was beginning a new life. Guinevere had tortured me enough over those past ten years. I told myself that if she wanted to lay with me, she would have to have me dragged into her chambers by my heels. From then on, I would live like other men and take my pleasures when and where I wished. I had a lot of catching up to do.

Chapter 16

Of all the ladies who lusted after me and all the knights who loved me as a brother, no one's love for me was stronger or stranger than that of Galehot.

Galehot was the only surviving son of an elderly King whose lands were far to the north of Arthur's domains. Born with a deformity of his back, Galehot was unable to train with or wield arms. Yet, he had a noble knight's devotion to honor and prowess. He greatly admired the knightly virtues, and since his father had great riches and denied him nothing, he drew into his company many great knights.

Stories of the prowess of Arthur's knights were told and sung of, far and wide, and when they reached Galehot, he was enthralled by the deeds of Tristan, Gawain, Lamorak, Bors, Percival and, yes, Lancelot. His mission in life became the need to test the prowess of his knights against Arthur's greatest warriors, and so he declared war and invaded Britain.

When word of the incursion reached Arthur in Londinium, he called a war council, which agreed that an army should be raised and assembled at Wroxeter by the following spring.

That May Arthur had a war camp built on the old Roman hill-fort that was called Viroconium. At first many barons and knights responded to his call to service, but as the days and weeks went by, the arrival of men slowed to a trickle and Arthur began to rage and curse at the lack of support from his own people.

For years, Arthur had neglected his sworn duties and obligations as a knight and as a King. The poor suffered increasingly so that the rich could benefit. The King showered riches on those who were already rich and taxed the poor to support his purchase of castles and lands and to make war as he saw fit. Even the law was made to benefit the rich and powerful, while the poor looked to knights like me for a bit of justice.

As a result, the rich barons thought themselves too important to rush to Arthur's battle flag, and the poor knights stayed at home tending their crops and cattle, trying to eke out enough to survive another winter.

As little as I wanted to, I answered Arthur's call and rode off from Joyous Garde with fifty of my knights, double that number of squires and thirty ox-drawn wagons loaded with food, weapons and all manner of supplies needed for a full-scale war. When we neared Wroxeter, I decided not to join Arthur's camp but to set up my own war camp in a nearby wooded area. We would support Arthur if we were needed, but we could remain hidden as long as we wished and not be under his flag.

It amused me more than a little to hear that Arthur raged and cursed with frustration at my absence. Nevertheless, I kept my presence secret and decided that when the time came for me to fight, I would wear someone else's armor and ride someone else's horse in order to hide my identity and continue to vex the King. Galehot's camp was less than a mile from Arthur's and only a wide but shallow stream with broad banks and open fields on both sides separated the two armies.

After much preparation and procrastination, the strangest war I had ever heard of finally began.

Galehot sent fifty knights into the stream to encounter with Arthur's knights. Arthur responded with one hundred knights. In spite of being outnumbered Galehot's knights not only held their own but, also, appeared to be getting the upper hand in the battle. Then, Gawain entered the fray, and because of his great prowess, the advantage swung back to Arthur's side, and Galehot's knights were forced to retreat.

Galehot sent in another one hundred knights and in spite of Gawain, the battle once again went to Galehot's advantage, and Arthur's knights retreated to avoid being overwhelmed.

I had been watching from a nearby rise and was already armed and mounted. When I saw Gawain being severely pressed and in grave danger, I galloped down the hill and into the melee.

My efforts seemed to make a difference, as Galehot's knights could not hold their line against me, and they turned and rode, as best they could, back to their own camp.

Through all of this, only knights had been in the battle and I was confused not only by the nature of the encounters but Galehot's failure to send more knights, foot soldiers or archers to attack me. For all intents and purposes, what we were having was an enormous tournament with jousting and general melees.

After the last encounter, which was violent but brief, there was no more fighting for the rest of the day. Gawain had received a number of injuries, but none of them was serious. I rode away from the field as soon as I could, and that evening there was much talk in both camps about the unknown knight who had wreaked such havoc and shown such prowess.

The next day was much like the first, except that the number of knights facing each other was greater. Gawain was, once again, magnificent in battle, but he had taken too many injuries and had to be carried off the field.

Once again, I entered the fray but this time on a different horse, wearing a different suit of armor and carrying a different shield. Again I was able to assist Arthur's knights enough to cause Galehot's men to retreat, leaving large numbers of their comrades dead or wounded on the grassy fields.

As I rode away towards our camp, a mounted gentleman blocked my path. He raised his hand in a gesture of peace as I approached him.

"Sir knight," he said, "my name is Galehot. I have searched for you all my life."

I had no idea what he meant, but I was surprised and intrigued.

Galehot's palfrey was more richly accoutered with gold and precious gems, than any I had ever seen. But, the man was himself simply and elegantly dressed without any adornment. His face was extremely handsome with bright, intelligent blue eyes and a strong but smiling mouth with straight, white teeth. There was strength in his arms, legs and large hands. There was no doubt that he would have been a formidable warrior if not for his back that forced him to sit twisted in his saddle.

As he spoke, there was no hint of self-pity in his voice, and he seemed to be a genuinely happy person.

"What may I do for you, my lord?" I asked.

"I have searched for a knight of your prowess in many countries and have found none until now. I beg you to join me in my pavilion, where you shall be treated to great comfort and honor, since I wish to know you and enjoy your company."

"My lord," I said, "I will go with you gladly, but I am King Arthur's liegeman and I must defend his honor and Kingdom when the battle resumes tomorrow."

"Sir Knight," Galehot replied, "my quest is fulfilled by your prowess and gallantry. There will be no further encounters, and I will withdraw my army to my own country, if you will consent to be my companion and accompany me for one year and if you consent to tell me your name."

"My lord, for the sake of all who might suffer or die in this war, I will do as you ask. As for my name, I am called Lancelot of the Lake and my father was King Ban of Benoic."

I have never seen a smile so great as the one on Galehot's face. As we rode, together, toward his camp, he would not stop talking about what he had seen me do and my prowess and generosity in battle.

Much has been said about Galehot and his strange love of men, but I never saw his behavior as anything other than proper, honorable and sinless. In the time I was with him, I came to understand that in spite of his outward good cheer, in his heart he harbored a great hopelessness born of his infirmity. He was his father's only son and he would be King in due time, but he could never be a knight. He would send men into battle to be maimed or killed, but he could never stand beside them and share their dangers, defeats and victories. But, he tried to share those experiences through the friendship and companionship of great knights. He hoped that, in some way, the knights he so loved, would induct him into their brotherhood, and then he could hold his head high with pride and count himself as a knight in spirit if not in body.

I spent a happy year with my lord Galehot, and it was indeed a sad day for both of us, when I rode away to go on with my life. Many in Arthur's camp believed it was I who had twice come to their rescue during the battle with Galehot. But, I would neither confirm nor deny any part in that fight, and I would not tell anyone where I had been for that year of my absence.

Years later, I heard that Galehot had died of sorrow when he was falsely told of my death in battle at Joyous Garde. The news affected me greatly. I had come to love him in the time we had spent together. I mourned him then and I still do.

Chapter 17

There are men whose ambition and greed for power leaves no place in their lives for honor and fidelity. Mordaunt was such a man. Whether he was Arthur's nephew or his son no longer mattered to the schemers and plotters in the King's court; they had made his cause theirs as well and they anxiously anticipated the time when he would be High King of Britain.

All that Mordaunt lacked in personal courage he more than made up for with deceit, dishonor, disloyalty and cunning. He realized that despite my resentment toward the King I would not allow him to be overthrown. I was the one who stood in Mordaunt's path but I might be convinced to step aside if Arthur was the cause of Guinevere's death.

It was soon after I returned to Arthur's court, after leaving Galehot, that Mordaunt and Agravaine began a plot to have Arthur sentence and kill the Queen for the crime of adultery and treason against the King.

Agravaine had a liegeman who was a knight by the name of Maleageant. He had brought the man, who was of common birth, out of poverty and had given him a decent life and opportunity to better himself. As a result, Maleageant owed everything to Agravaine and would do anything that his benefactor asked of him.

Maleageant had developed into an incredibly big and strong man. Combined with the quickness and cunning of a wild animal, total fearlessness and brutal aggression, he had been the victor in every battle he had fought on Agravaine's behalf. He had received excellent training, and had greater prowess with the lance and sword, than most other knights of noble birth.

Agravaine and Mordaunt chose the time and place to cause mischief when Arthur's court was at Carlisle and I was far away at Joyous Garde with Lionel, Bors and Percival. Gawain's whereabouts were known only to the gods.

Fortunately, the schemers did not recognize young Sir Cael of Gwent who was a witness to their dishonorable proceedings. Nor did they count on his loyalty and intelligence.

One morning, Agravaine brought Maleageant to the assizes, where the King was hearing legal cases.

"My lord," said Agravaine, "this is my liegeman, Sir Maleageant. It is with great sadness that I must bring him before you with an accusation of treason against you. I would not do so if I did not have great trust and faith in Sir Maleageant's honesty."

"Sir Maleageant," said Arthur, "come forward and speak openly and freely without fear of reproach. But I warn you, if you cannot prove your accusation, you will have to defend yourself on the field of battle. God alone knows all truths, and He will reveal the truth to us through your victory or your death."

"My lord, I have no fear of death in this cause. I had a knight, named Sir Aglent, who bragged to me that he had lain many times with your wife the Queen, my Lady Guinevere. I called him a liar, but he showed me many gifts that he said she had given him. I recognized some of the Queen's rings and brooches that I have seen with my own eyes when I had the high honor of attending you in your Great Hall."

Cael told me that Arthur's face turned deathly pale at this public accusation, and that everyone within earshot began yelling and cursing. Fighting broke out between the Queen's defenders and those who thought the worst of her and wanted her deposed or murdered.

Somehow, Arthur was able to contain his anger. He stood up from his chair, raised his arms and shouted for order. When quiet was restored, he turned his attention to Maleageant.

"Where is Sir Aglent? I wish to question him. Why have you not brought him to me to confirm or deny your accusations?"

"My lord," said Maleageant, "I would have brought him here by force, but he resisted me, and I slew him as he defended himself."

"There is no choice then," said Arthur, "you must defend the truth of your accusation in battle. The Queen shall choose a champion, whom you shall fight to the death at high noon tomorrow. If the Queen's champion fails to appear or is defeated, she will be found guilty of treason against the High King of Britain, and she will die by beheading forthwith."

I will not accuse the King of collusion in this plot against Guinevere. Nevertheless, he knew that I was at Joyous Garde, and his mark of one day made it appear impossible for messengers to reach me or Gawain (if anyone knew where he was) and for either of us to return in time to save her.

But as soon as the sentence was proclaimed, Cael ran to his quarters and, gathering all of his squires and pages, he explained, with a sense of great urgency, the plans he had already formed.

Cael had three squires and three pages who were old enough and experienced for hard riding. He had them mounted on the fastest and hardiest palfreys and sped them off toward Joyous Garde, while he remained in Carlisle.

Cael knew the distance between Carlisle and Joyous Garde was eighty miles. He instructed each squire and page to stop and remain at a chosen relay point. The last rider would reach Joyous Garde while the other horses at the five stages could rest, regain their strength and be ready for me.

The last rider appeared at Joyous Garde with the first rays of the sun. It required only minutes for him to explain what had happened and the route I was to take to reach Carlisle. Anger and hatred rose up in me, but I forced myself to remain calm. I ordered the fastest horse in my stable to be saddled, without delay, and then I was gone without even a sword to weigh him down.

I rode as hard and as fast as I could, caring only that the horse would not fall or injure a leg. It was still early morning when I drew the lathered and panting palfrey to a sliding halt at the first station. The page was waiting for me with his horse's reins at the ready. I dismounted and leaped onto the lad's palfrey. I nodded my deep felt thanks to him and without a word, I thundered away again.

I continued on the road that had been laid out for me and four more times I changed horses and pushed on, without a moment's rest or a morsel of food, knowing that the Queen's life, and Cael's life, depended on my arrival before the sun was at its zenith.

The exhausted palfrey was stumbling, but, somehow, he carried me through the streets of Carlisle and into the lists near the King's villa. The sun was directly overhead. I slid to the ground and saw everything in a quick glance. Guinevere stood forlornly alone in the center of the field. The King sat on a raised platform surrounded by Agravaine, Gaheris, Mordaunt and all of their cronies. They were all armed to the teeth. There was no sign of Gawain or Gareth.

A very big and strong looking knight was sitting on a huge destrier at one end of the lists. He was well armed, and I took him to be the Maleageant who had accused the Queen.

Finally, there was my young hero Sir Cael, mounted and in armor and prepared to defend the Queen, if I did not appear in time.

I ignored the shouting of those who had come to see the Queen saved or murdered and walked toward Cael who had dismounted and was so happy to see me that I could not help smiling in spite of the deathly seriousness of our situation. He would not allow any of his squires to touch me but he was quickly disarmed, and then he armed me, as he had done so often in earlier times. I saw his eyes misting and for a moment, I allowed myself the wonderful feeling of love I had for him and his brothers, Brendan and Loegaire. I knew in that instant that they would have done the same for me if they had been in Cael's place.

Then I pulled my thoughts away from happy nostalgia and turned to the business at hand.

I mounted Cael's very fine destrier, couched his lance and galloped directly at my foe. He was alert and ready and charged as well. I was at a slight disadvantage, not being familiar with my mount. Nevertheless, I gave a good accounting of myself and we each shattered a lance on our shields. Squires ran up with two more lances, and we charged each other again. He was a big man and gripped the saddle well, but this time both of us were unhorsed. I got to my feet, threw my shield to the ground and attacked him with my sword. He had never fought anyone as strong as me, but I had fought Tristan, and Maleageant was no Sir Tristan.

I beat on his shield without pause, and he had such difficulty defending himself from my onslaught that he had no chance to bring his sword into play. Finally, he dropped his guard for an instant and Cael's sword sliced through his helmet and into his skull. He fell to the ground, already dead.

Through all of this, I had heard only the sound of blood pounding in my ears. Now, I heard the cheering of the mob surrounding the King. I removed my helmet, threw it to the ground and remounted my horse. I walked the destrier toward the King, until I was close enough to look down on him. I am sure that anger and hatred showed on my face, but he did not see it. He stared, without blinking, past me and at the Queen, his jaws clenched and not one word spoken.

I turned the horse and rode over to Guinevere. I lifted her to the saddle in front of me and trotted over to where Cael and his entourage were still celebrating.

It amused me to think that if Merlin were still alive he would have been delighted with Cael's strategy of setting relays. Still, he would have convinced everyone that I had been transported from Joyous Garde to Carlisle by his magic.

I had proven Guinevere's innocence by slaughtering her accuser, and Arthur had no choice but to accept God's verdict. But of course, he had never believed the accusation in the first place. Unfortunately, nothing had really changed. It was obvious to the entire court that Guinevere's life was in danger. Agravaine and Mordaunt would not stop at one failure, and Arthur abandoned any pretext of caring for his wife and defending her innocence. He had cut the last string of attachment to me and was now fully committed to his nephew's success.

The Queen's situation was terrible. She no longer sat near Arthur at meals, and I was relegated to a corner of the Great Hall. My cousins and liegemen were furious with the King, and they constantly urged me to leave the court and take Guinevere with me if I wished. They had no reluctance to support me against the King. An insult to me was an insult to all of the knights who supported me, and they were the proudest knights in Arthur's court. They wanted war, and that was the reason why I would not leave the court, no matter what the provocation. My loss of pride was a small price to pay for avoiding the great loss of life, the destruction of Arthur's court and perhaps the collapse of united Britain. I also feared for good friends, like Gareth and Percival, who would be caught between loyalty to the King and love for me.

As time went by, Guinevere and I became closer. Many who had been her friends and companions, drifted away from her because of the King's enmity. She was afraid to sleep, and when exhaustion overtook her, she had frightening dreams of being burned at the stake. She begged me to stay with her day and night, as I was the only one she felt truly safe with. I knew that we could not go on living the way we were, but I could not bring myself to make a final break with Arthur and take his Queen from him.

It was not long before Agravaine and Mordaunt hatched another plot while the court was at Carlisle Castle.

They convinced the King to leave the court to go hunting and to make sure that Gawain accompanied him. To assure that Guinevere would have no reason to refuse my visit they also wanted the Queen to be informed of the King's plans to remain at his hunting camp over night, They intended to wait until I went to the Queen's lodging as I did whenever I could. As soon as I was in her rooms they would attack and take the two of us prisoner. Then they would accuse us both of treasonous adultery whether we were lying together or not. They swore to the King that they would bring me to him dead or alive and that he would finally be rid of me and his wife.

Arthur agreed with the plan but warned them to take enough men with them since I was unlikely to be captured without a fight.

Agravaine promised that he and Mordaunt would take twelve other knights who had reason to hate me. They would be sufficient to overwhelm me especially since I would be unarmed and fearful of injury to the Queen.

That evening, when I told Bors that I was ready to go see the Queen, he was particularly concerned. If I believed in such things, I would say that he had a premonition.

"Cousin," said Bors, "Agravaine and his cohorts have been spying on you and the Queen. They will do what they can to bring shame and dishonor on you and all of your kin. I have never felt as strongly as I do tonight that you should not go to her. I believe that the King is staying outside of the castle tonight because he has set someone to spy on you. I fear a trap."

"Do not worry," I said. "I will talk with her for a little while, and then return here."

"Then go," said Bors, "and come back safe and sound."

So, I left Bors and carried my sword under my arm wrapped in a cape. But, I wore no armor. When I reached the outer door to the Queen's chambers, which was neither locked nor bolted, I entered quietly. Guinevere was waiting for me. We embraced and passed through to a second, inner chamber. Within minutes, Agravaine, Mordaunt and twelve other knights burst through the outer door screaming "traitor" at the top of their lungs.

I suppose that I was particularly alert because of Bors' warning, and at the first sounds, I leaped to the door of the inner chamber and barred it.

"Madam," I shouted above the din, "I regret that our love has brought us to a terrible end. There must be many knights on the other side of this door, and I have no armor."

"Alas," moaned the Queen, "you cannot defend yourself. You will be killed, and I will be burned at the stake."

Meanwhile, Agravaine and Mordaunt continued to yell, "Traitor knight, come out. You cannot escape."

As the seconds went by, I became more and more enraged. Surrender was out of the question. I had been anxiously pacing back and forth like a caged animal.

"I cannot stand this any longer," I roared. "I would rather die than let them take me without fighting."

I took Guinevere in my arms and kissed her and said, "Guinevere, my Queen, I beg you to pray for me. And do not fear. I promise you, that if I am killed, Bors and all of my kin will not fail to rescue you, and you shall live like a Queen on my lands."

"Lancelot," she replied, "you know that if you are killed, I will die as well."

"Well, madam, then this is the day that our love ends."

I wrapped my cape around my left arm, grasped my sword in my right hand and moved to the door.

"Fair lords," I cried out loudly, "stop your shouting and banging and I shall open the door."

"Come on then and do it," answered Agravaine, "it makes no sense for you to fight and die. Let us in, and we will take you alive to King Arthur."

I unbarred the door and as it opened inward, the crowd of knights pushed the knight who was closest to the opening into the chamber. I saw my chance, pushed back against the door with all of my strength and barred the door again.

Sir Colgrevance was a big, strong knight, and when he regained his balance, he struck hard at me. But, I parried the blow with my wrapped left arm, and with my sword, struck the knight's helmet so hard that he fell dead on the chamber floor.

In an instant, the outcome of this fight was no longer so sure. With Guinevere's help, I armed myself quickly in Colgrevance's armor. And, still, Agravaine, Mordaunt and eleven other knights stood outside the chamber, now threatening to kill me.

"Stop your noise," I shouted, "you shall not take me tonight. Take my advice and leave. I promise you that if you go, I will appear before you and the King tomorrow morning. Then any or all of you can accuse me of treason, and I will defend myself as any knight should."

"Fie on you, traitor knight," replied Agravaine. "The King has given us the choice of bringing you to him dead or alive. We will take you and kill you now."

"Well, then," said Lancelot, "if there is no honor in you, look to yourselves."

This was not the first time I had faced so many knights in combat. I flung the door open and, in a raging fury, crashed into the crowd of knights waiting for me. With the first swing of my arm, I split Agravaine's head and killed him instantly. Then hurling myself first one way and then the other, I thrashed and hacked with that bloody sword, until twelve knights lay dead in the small chamber. Only Mordaunt, who was wounded, managed to escape.

I looked around at what I had done, and was immediately overcome with regret and sadness.

"Madam," I said quietly to the Queen, "you know that what I have done here will not be forgiven. Our love is ended, but if you will come with me now to Joyous Garde, I will protect you from all danger."

"That is not for the best," said the Queen. "Let us see what happens, now that you have killed these knights who were your worst enemies. If you see tomorrow morning that they will put me to death, you may come and rescue me, as you think best."

"That I will do without fail," I said.

Then we exchanged gold rings, and I left the Queen and returned to my own lodgings.

Bors, Lionel and several other knights from Brittany had gathered in my rooms. They were greatly relieved, but surprised to see me in someone else's armor. Their mood changed when I told them what had happened.

"My friends," I said, "I regret that I have brought misfortune to all of you, but I did what I was forced to do against my will. I hope that you will forgive me and meet whatever comes with strength and courage, for I believe that now we are at war."

"Sir," said Bors, "whatever fate sends us, is welcome. We have had much honor and good fortune with you, and we will take misfortune with you as well. Look around you and take comfort. There is no group of knights who can do us more harm than we can do to them."

"Thank you," I said, "I am in your debt. But, I must ask a favor of you, dear cousin, that you must do quickly. It will not take long for word to spread about the battle, even in the dark of night. Find out who among the knights will support me and who will not. I must know who are my friends and who are my enemies."

"Sir," said Bors, "I shall do my best, and before it is mid-morning, we shall know who will stand with you."

By morning, Bors had assembled nineteen knights who were my kin or friends. They were joined by eighty other knights, who had been allied with Sir Lamorak or Sir Tristan, and had reason to seek vengeance against the King or the sons of Lot.

When they had gathered together, I said, "My lords, you all know that since I came to this country, I have fought for and defended King Arthur and Queen Guinevere. Last night, I went to sit with the Queen, as I always do, but the King ordered my betrayal, and I am now accused of treason. In my own defense, I killed Sir Agravaine and twelve of his kin and friends, and now, I am sure, that war will be waged against me and mine. The King is angry and full of malice. He will judge the Queen to be guilty and will sentence her to the fire. I will not allow her to be burned. I will fight for the Queen, but what will you do?"

"We will do as you will do," they all shouted.

I asked all of my followers to arm themselves and, when they were ready, to ride with me to a small wood near the castle, where we could hide and wait to see what the King would do.

What I tell you now, Lonmarch, is based on neither lie nor conjecture. Some of what I can relate is of my own knowledge but there is much I did not witness. However, Sir Pelleas, a brave knight, trusted and loved by Arthur, was witness to all that transpired between Arthur and his nephews. When there was no longer any liege lord, cause or honor left for him to defend, Sir Pelleas reported to me all that he had seen and heard. I will honestly and without guile relate to you all that I know and have been told.

When Mordaunt escaped from the slaughter in the Queen's chamber, he ran to his horse and rode, wounded and bleeding, to King Arthur's camp. There he told Arthur and Gawain, who attended the King with his brothers Gaheris and Gareth, what had happened and that he was the only survivor.

"How can this be?" moaned the King, "you had him trapped in the Queen's chamber."

"I swear that is the truth," Mordaunt whined. "We found him unarmed except for his sword. But, he killed Colgrevance and took his armor."

"Ah, he is a marvelous knight of great prowess. Alas that now he will be my enemy. Nevertheless, the Queen must be put to death for treason or I will be dishonored."

Gawain held up his hand and said, "My lord, do not be so hasty in your judgment against the Queen. Lancelot may not have been in the Queen's chambers for any evil purpose. You know, my lord, that the Queen is much in debt to Lancelot. He has saved her life and done battle for her when everyone else refused to help. Perhaps she sent for him to reward him for his good deeds in private to avoid any slanderous gossip. Sometimes things we do for the best turn out for the worst. I believe that your Queen is faithful to you. As for Lancelot, he will prove his innocence, and the Queen's as well, on the field of battle against any knight you choose."

"That I believe," said the King, "but this time, I will not allow Lancelot to fight for the Queen. This time, I am sentencing her to death according to the law. And if I get my hands on Lancelot, I will sentence him to burn as well."

"I pray that I will never live to see that," said Gawain.

"Why do you say that?" asked the King. "You have no cause to defend Lancelot. Last night, he killed your brother Agravaine and wounded Mordaunt. He killed twelve other knights as well."

"My lord," answered Gawain, "I know about all those deaths and I regret them. But I warned them. I told them what would happen in the end. Since they would not listen to my advice, I will not meddle in what happens next or seek revenge. No matter how sorry I am, they were responsible for their own deaths."

"Nevertheless," Arthur said, "I want you to put on your best armor and, with your brothers, Gaheris and Gareth, take the Queen to the stake to receive her judgment and be burned to death."

"No, my lord," said Gawain, "that I will never do. I will never be a witness to such a shameful end for so noble a lady as Dame Guinevere. My heart will not allow me to see her die, and I will not have it said that I took part in her death."

"Then," said the King, "allow your brothers Gaheris and Gareth to be there."

"My lord," said Gawain with great bitterness, "they will be reluctant to do what you ask, but they are unable to refuse you."

Gaheris remained silent, but Sir Gareth spoke up and said to Arthur, "Sir, you may command me to be there, but it shall be against my will. Unless you command me, I will not do as you wish. And if I must, I will go in peace and wear no armor nor carry a shield or sword."

"Then prepare yourselves," said the King angrily. "Soon, she shall have her judgment."

"Alas," said Gawain, "that I have lived to see this terrible day." Then he turned away from the King with tears in his eyes.

The next morning, the Queen was brought out to a field beside the Castle Carlisle where she was to be executed. Her fine clothes were torn off, so that only a thin smock was left to cover her body, and she was tied to a post that had been placed in the ground. She stood, unsteadily, on logs and kindling that were piled around and under her. Those who saw her remarked later about her calm expression and marveled at her bravery in the face of a horrible death.

Arthur and Mordaunt were sure that I would make some effort to rescue the Queen. They had gathered a large force of armed knights to ensure the success of the execution, but there was also much weeping and wailing among the lords and ladies who loved her. Meanwhile, her husband sat hidden in his chambers in the castle, where he would not witness the sentence he had imposed.

I had asked Sir Cael to remain in the castle, determine Arthur's plans and watch over the Queen. When he saw Guinevere stripped to her smock, he raced to where we were hidden in the woods. Upon hearing the news, we mounted and galloped at full speed back toward the castle and onto the field where Guinevere stood.

Arthur's knights, most on foot and only a few mounted, were tightly grouped in a circle around the Queen. We careened into them and the carnage was terrible. I was filled with blind rage as I hacked and hewed at everyone within reach.

Arthur and Mordaunt had seriously underestimated the strength of our numbers. We were one hundred mounted knights against forty or fifty. We encircled them, and every knight who stood his ground against us was wounded or killed.

When the slaughter was over, I rode straight to Guinevere, cut her bonds and lifted her up behind me onto my horse. Then my knights and I rode to Joyous Garde.

As we rode away, I was unaware of the great horror that had befallen all of us. In the melee, as I hacked and slashed my way through the crowd of Arthur's knights, I had killed Sir Gaheris and Sir Gareth, even though Gareth was unarmed. In my anger and frenzy, I had not recognized them, and now, they lay covered by the bodies of many others who had been killed or injured.

When word of the Queen's rescue and the deaths of Gaheris and Gareth reached the King, at first he was stunned, Then he began his public lamentation and the placement of blame. He stormed and raged. He pulled his hair and tore his shirt and wailed long enough and loud enough for everyone to hear, "Agravaine, oh Agravaine, may God forgive you for the evil you have done."

One of Arthur's knights went to Gawain and told him how the Queen was rescued and that twenty-four knights had been killed.

"I knew," said Gawain, "that Lancelot would rescue her or die in the attempt. To tell the truth, he would not have been a man of honor if he had not rescued her, since she would have died for his sake. But where are my brothers?"

"Sir Gareth and Sir Gaheris have been killed," whispered the knight.

"How can that be? Who killed them?" Gawain shouted.

"Sir," the knight answered, "Lancelot killed them both."

"Alas," cried Gawain, "all the joy in my life is gone," and he fell to the ground in a faint and lay there as if he were dead. When his eyes finally opened, Gawain began to weep bitterly and for a long while remained where he was, crying and moaning. Then, when he was able to compose himself, he rose and went to the King.

When he approached the King, he began to sob again and cried out, "Oh, King Arthur, my uncle, my brother Gareth is dead and so is my brother Gaheris. My lord, tell me how Lancelot killed my brothers."

"I will tell you everything that was told to me," said the King.

There are many places in this land, and even foreign lands, where the names Lancelot and Guinevere are cursed for bringing death and destruction to the court of King Arthur and, because of that, the end of peace and unity in Britain. I deem it of no use to argue for my innocence and honor, since those who are against me will call me liar and those who are for me need no excuses or explanations. I do swear, however, that the Queen had never committed adultery with me.

In truth, all that befell Arthur after that terrible day was a result of his own falsehoods and manipulation. When Gawain asked his uncle how his brothers had died, the King could have told the truth and said that I did not recognize Gareth and Gaheris in the midst of the battle and that I did not know what I had done. But, instead of trying to calm Gawain, he said that I slew them out of malice and intended to destroy them for my own gain.

Then the King urged Gawain to avenge their deaths. "Nephew," he said, "Lancelot will wait for us at Joyous Garde and many kings and knights will go to his side, but we shall have the greater force and we shall prevail."

"That I believe," said Gawain sadly, "therefore count your friends and I will count mine."

"That shall be done," the King replied, "and I am sure that we will have enough strength on our side to force him out of the biggest tower in his castle."

So, the King sent messengers throughout Britain to summon all of his knights to war. And, when all of the knights, dukes, and earls came together, he had a great army, which marched to make war on me and mine at Joyous Garde.

Chapter 18

I had not been idle in my stewardship of Joyous Garde. The castle, being on a hill with the North Sea at its eastern base, was well protected from any hostile force. However, the town, which is on the flat plain beginning at the base of the hill, was open and vulnerable to an invading army. The people in outlying farms and settlements had never had a safe haven to retreat to in times of war. For that reason, when I first became the master of Joyous Garde, I had ordered the construction of a defensive ditch and wall, including new hill forts to surround the town. At the height of five men, built solidly of rock and stone and topped with a wide rampart, the wall was easily defensible. There were four gates that were too small for a mounted knight to enter, and only one massive gate, which was strong enough to resist any attack.

In the event of war, my people could take refuge in the town. Underground springs assured a continuous supply of fresh water and our storage buildings were stocked with grain, dried meat and fish, cheese, beans, salt, honey and vinegar. We had a good supply of grain and fodder for animals that would supply us with fresh meat, and we also stocked a large supply of malt to make beer. We were prepared for a long siege, if that were ever necessary.

Satisfying the needs of one hundred knights, more than three hundred squires and pages and all of their horses was a monumental task. I thanked the gods every day for Sir Gregoire, his son and the many attendants who worked for them. They arranged for lodging and feeding everyone and even planned games, music and amusements to occupy so many men who were bred and trained for action and excitement.

As time went by it became harder to bear the thought of all out war and a general slaughter of the knights whom I had called friend and broken bread with so many times over the years. But, at the same time, I could not ask my people to endure the suffering of a long siege. They would lose their homes, farms and livestock and if I was defeated they would be thrown into poverty or, even worse, sold into slavery.

Word came quickly about Arthur's plans, and we made final preparations in the city and castle to face his forces. But, when news came of the size of the King's army, we realized that the force arrayed against us was too great to match him in battle on an open field. We had barely one hundred knights. Arthur had threefold that number and at least one thousand foot soldiers and an equal number of archers. There was no choice for us but to face a long siege.

In the first days after Arthur arrived and set up his camp, there were brief skirmishes between both parties, but I would not allow my knights to ride out of the castle, and the siege went on for fifteen weeks.

One day, under a flag of truce, I rode out onto the plain at the bottom of the hill and called to Arthur and Gawain. They mounted their horses and rode up to me.

"My lords," I said, "your siege is in vain and none of us will gain any honor by it. I beg you to put an end to this war."

"That I will never do," the King growled. "But the siege will end now if you have the courage to fight me here in the middle of the field."

"Never," I said, "I will not fight against the King who made me a knight."

"Fie on your pretty talk," the King retorted, "I am your mortal foe until the day that I die. You have killed my kin and my friends and you have been my wife's lover and, like a traitor, you have taken her from me by force."

The King's words stung like sword strokes. In the past I would have rushed at him like a madman and killed him on the spot. But, now, I held myself in check. I forced myself to remember that their words could not stain my honor or prowess. My duty was to protect and defend my home, my people and those I loved.

"My lord," I answered, "you may say what you wish, for you know I will not fight you. You say that I have killed your family and friends. Well, I have done that and I regret it with all my heart, but I was forced to defend myself or lose my life. As for my lady, Dame Guinevere, she has been a true wife to you. However, she has had the good grace and kindness to hold me dear and cherish me more than any other knight. I have deserved her love, my lord, for you in your hate and anger have sought to prove her guilt and to have her killed or burned at the stake. I have defended her innocence and her accusers have died for their lies. It would have been dishonorable for me, as a knight, if I had allowed the Queen to die for my sake. Since I have fought battles for her when they were not my quarrels, it was only right for me to fight for her when she was condemned because of your quarrel with me. Therefore, my lord, I ask you to take your Queen back into your good graces, for she is fair, good and true."

"Fie on you, false traitor knight" growled Gawain, "my uncle shall have his way with you and the Queen in spite of your fine words, and he will kill you both as it pleases him."

"That may well be," I answered, "but if I decide to come out of this castle and deal with you, you may have a harder time taking me and the Queen than you have ever had."

"Fie on your brave words, you false traitor knight," Gawain yelled, "why did you kill my brother Gareth, when he loved you more than his own kin? You made him a knight with your own hands. Why did you kill the one who loved you so much?"

"There is nothing that I can say to excuse what I have done," I answered sadly. "My regret is as great as if I had killed my own cousin, Sir Bors. But, alas, I never did see Sir Gareth and Sir Gaheris."

"You lie," Gawain screamed, "you killed them because you hate me. Therefore, I will make war on you as long as I live."

"I regret that," I said, "but I know that there is no way to make peace with you as long as your heart is set on revenge. But if it were not for your hatred of me, I am sure that I could make peace with the King."

"I believe that, you false knight," Gawain replied, "for you are a liar and have always misled the King. But this time we all can see that you have dishonorably killed our knights."

"You may say what you wish," I answered, "but I have never killed a knight by treason as you have done."

"Ah, cowardly knight," Gawain retorted angrily. "If you mean Sir Lamorak, you lie. You know that I killed him honorably." "That cannot be," I said. "You had help in killing him. He was too great a knight for you to have beaten him by yourself."

"Well, well," said Gawain, "since you now accuse me of murdering Lamorak, I will never give up until I have you in my hands."

I realized that no good could be gained by further talk, and turned my horse back up the hill and through the castle gate.

I saw very little of Guinevere. She spent her days praying in her own little chapel and took her meals with her ladies, apart from me. One day she came to me, her eyes red from crying.

"Lancelot," she said, "you must end this war. Return me to my husband so that he may do with me what he will and this siege will end. I cannot continue to watch the killing every day and if I must die for the sake of peace between you and the King I will gladly go to him."

"Dear Guinevere," I answered, "if returning you to the King would end this struggle I would do so even at the cost of my own life. But that will not happen. It is not a simple matter of making peace between me and the King. Mordaunt is determined to be King. He urges Gawain to resist any condition of peace and Arthur will do as Gawain wishes. He intends for me to kill Gawain and the King. Then his path to the throne will be clear and he can raise an army to deal with me. I have only two choices. I must fight now or wait and hope that some event will cause Arthur to raise this siege. But in any case I will not exchange your life for peace between Arthur and me.

As I spoke, the Queen's demeanor became more and more depressed. With one long, last look at me she turned away and left me alone. I did not see her for days after that and we spoke not at all.

My knights spent their days doing what knights do when they are confined to small spaces. They practiced at arms almost constantly, trying to kill their boredom before they killed each other. I ordered jousts and tournaments to occupy them but I was careful to prevent the formation of factions that might become too competitive and deadly. Being confined ito the castle grounds was unnatural and there were frequent forays into the town where they caroused and drank in the inns, which prospered greatly under the circumstances. Their need to fight grew more intense as time went by and their pride and vigor were getting too great to assuage with games and practice. I realized that I could not maintain a siege in which the best knights of Britain were restrained like caged animals.

As for me, I followed a routine that never changed. After the morning meal I walked the full perimeter of the wall surrounding the castle and town. I inspected the sentries and the condition of the wall itself and issued orders, which a scribe, who accompanied me, wrote down for others to carry out. I could have performed this task on horseback but I chose to be on every man's level, to look him in the eye, to speak words of assurance and encouragement and to be alert to signs of fear or hopelessness that could undermine our resistance.

It was during these rounds that I learned of new marriages, new babes born, illnesses and deaths. I also learned that the people had great confidence in me, and they trusted that in the end, we would prevail. The more I came to know the people of every station the more I was determined to protect them from death or slavery.

In spite of my orders, one or more of my knights found their way out of the castle each day to fight against Arthur's knights. Usually they were evenly matched and there would be injuries and deaths on each side. After such encounters the squires and litter bearers would rush out to collect the dead and wounded.

All too often Gawain came out to fight. None of my knights could overcome him but they fought him out of pride and to defend my honor. It was heart wrenching to see my friends fall each day but I could not bring myself to fight Gawain. Nor would I raise a hand against the King.

In the mean time, Gawain had told his men to whistle and hoot at me, and they began to yell insults at me and called me a coward and villain. When Bors, Ector, and Lionel heard the noise coming from Gawain's men, they gathered Sir Palomides, Sir Safere and Sir Lavaine and many more of their kin and friends and sought me out.

"My lord," said Bors, "we can no longer tolerate the lies and insults we have heard from Gawain. We beg you to free us from these castle walls and let us ride into the field to fight our enemies. All your reasoning and kind words will not do any good. Sir Gawain will not allow you to make peace with the King. Therefore, you must fight for your rights and your honor."

"Alas," I said. "I am reluctant to fight, but I will not deny your request, since we cannot delay with honor." I went back to the castle walls and called down to Arthur and Gawain, "My lords, I have decided that since everyone wishes to fight, I will comply with your request and we will ride into the field tomorrow morning."

So, each side prepared itself, and I was told later that Gawain called a group of knights to him and ordered them to find me in the midst of the battle, overwhelm me and kill me.

At midmorning, the King was already in the field. Our knights came out to meet Arthur's formation. Before the general melee, Gawain lowered his spear in a challenge to joust. Lionel spurred his horse quickly to meet Gawain. As their horses collided, with both armies looking on, Gawain pierced Lionel through the body with his lance. As Lionel fell to the ground, only slightly wounded, Sir Palomides and his knights rushed forward to rescue him and carry him to the castle. Then the great battle began.

Many knights and fighting men were wounded or killed on both sides. Sir Bors, together with my other kin and close friends, wreaked havoc and great slaughter against King Arthur's side.

Through it all, I would not fight against Arthur's side, but I did what I could to protect my own people from his knights. Yet, Arthur did everything he could to get close to me, and when he did, I defended myself but would not strike back.

Finally, Bors challenged the King and, with a spear, struck Arthur from his horse. Bors dismounted and ran to the King with his sword raised to kill him. "Shall I put an end to this war?" Bors yelled to me over the noise of battle.

"Hold your hand," I shouted. "I can not bear to see the King shamed or killed."

I leaped from my horse, helped the King to his feet, and lifted him up into the saddle of my own horse. I held the horse's bridle, looked up at the King's face and said, "My lord, stop this war. You will gain no honor here. I could do my best against you, but I hold back while you do not hold back against me. Remember, my lord, what I have done for you so many times and how evilly you now repay me."

Arthur looked down at me with tears in his eyes. "Alas," he said, "that this war ever began." Then he turned from me and rode away.

By then both armies had withdrawn to rest, tend to their wounded and remove the dead for burial. The armies remained camped on the field of battle that night, and by midmorning of the next day, they prepared to resume the fight.

When the war trumpets sounded, knights on both sides mounted their horses and rushed towards each other. Once again, Bors led the charge, and when he and Gawain saw each other, they braced their spears and crashed together with such force, that they were both thrown from their horses and lay injured on the ground. I saw what happened and rode quickly to my cousin. I lifted him onto my horse, and carried him to safety in the castle. Then the great battle was joined again and there was much slaughter on both sides.

In the castle, Sir Lavaine and Sir Urre came to me and pleaded with me to fight my enemies with all of my strength.

"Alas," I said, "I have no heart to fight against my King."

Sir Palomides came forward and said, "My lord, though you hold back and spare them, they will never forgive you. If they manage to surround you, they will murder you without mercy."

How many times had I said I would never fight against Arthur? If I changed my mind, I would be a liar and bring dishonor on myself. Still, I could no longer ignore the truth. We were greatly outnumbered, and if the fighting continued to go on, everyone I loved would be killed or imprisoned. I had only two choices. Either I had to surrender to the King and beg for terms of leniency for those who fought for me, or I had to fight to defend them and myself as well. I thought about Lionel and Bors lying wounded and all the deaths suffered on my side and I could not continue to spend their lives in return for my honor. Finally, I turned to my knights and said, "I will hold back no longer."

When we returned to the battle, I fought with all the power and fury that was within me. I rushed madly into the thickest part of every battle. I hacked and hewed at the enemy around me with such ferocity that knights and foot soldiers alike scurried away and fled for safety. Soon we were clearly winning the battle, and for pity's sake, I allowed the King's forces to withdraw. Then I called my own people into the castle to rest, treat the wounded and bury the dead.

With Gawain injured from his encounter with Bors, King Arthur's party was not as anxious as it had been before to go into battle, and both sides agreed to a temporary truce.

While the King's attention was turned to war, his kingdom began to suffer. Law and order was abandoned in many places and many people, rich and poor, refused to pay the taxes that had to be raised to meet the costs of the siege. Many barons and knights, who had joined Arthur, had left their families, castles and farms with no one to protect or manage them. Outlaws were free to burn and pillage, and hunger and homelessness began to spread among the people. As the affairs of the country grew worse, a group of clergymen gathered in Canterbury and selected the

Bishop of Rochester to go to the King and warn him about the state of the kingdom.

When the bishop came to Arthur, he told the King what was happening, and that the clergy and the people wanted him to forgive Guinevere, accept her again as his lawful Queen, and to make peace with Lancelot.

Arthur was well aware of the state of his kingdom and, since he needed an excuse to end the war, he was anxious to comply with the bishop's wishes. But, though Gawain was willing to accept forgiveness for the Queen, he would not agree to peace with me. After much discussion, the bishop realized that Gawain would not give up his hatred for me and that the King would continue to let Gawain have his way. So, the bishop had to be satisfied with part of what he had come to accomplish. He had Arthur write a letter promising me safe conduct to bring the Queen back to him. The letter also promised that he would never accuse her of treason or condemn her for anything that happened in the past. Then the bishop brought the King's letter to me and demanded that I bring the Queen to the King.

"It was never my intention to withhold the Queen," I said to the bishop, "but since she would have been killed for my sake, it was my responsibility to save her life. And now, since you have made peace, I will be a thousand times happier to take her back than I ever was to take her away. Go back to the King and tell him that in eight days I will bring my lady, Queen Guinevere, back to him."

I do believe that those eight days were the worst time in my life. I felt as if each day brought me one day closer to my death and all the joy in my life was bleeding out of me. I was sure that I would never see

Guinevere again and that the only real love I had in my life was ending. For her part, the Queen refused to see me during that time, but I know that she cried almost constantly and hardly ate or drank. My despair and misery grew almost too great to bear until I started to think about killing the Queen and myself. But that would have been the act of a coward. So, eight days later, as I promised, the Queen, one hundred knights and I rode out of the castle gates toward the King who waited outside of his war camp. I wore no armor, but my knights were armed to the teeth.

When we came before the King, I dismounted and helped the Queen from her horse. Then I led her by the arm to where the King stood among Sir Gawain and many other knights. Guinevere and I knelt down in front of the King, but he stood scowling and said nothing.

Since he would not acknowledge me, I stood up, raising the Queen with me.

"My most noble lord," I said, "I have brought you my lady, the Queen, as you have the right to require me to do. If there is any knight who dares to say that she has been unfaithful to you, I will prove upon his life that he is a liar. Anyone who has told you tales about the Queen is a liar. I went to the Queen as her friend and companion, not as her lover. I was no sooner inside her chambers, than Sir Agravaine, Sir Mordaunt and twelve other knights attacked me, calling me traitor and coward."

"They called you by the right name," growled Gawain.

"My lord, Sir Gawain," I said calmly, "in their quarrel with me they proved themselves wrong.

"My lord Arthur, I have given you no cause to wrong me as you have. My kin and I have served you better than any other knights. As for you, my lord Gawain, in battles, both on horseback and on foot, I have rescued you and your knights many times. I remind you how I rescued you from King Carados. Remember how I fought his brother, Sir Turquine, and killed him and freed your brother, Sir Gaheris, and sixty-four of my lord Arthur's knights from prison. You ought to remember these things, and that I deserve your good will and the King's good favor."

"The King may do as he wishes," said Gawain, "but you and I shall never be friends while we live. You have killed three of my brothers, and one of them you killed like a coward, for he was unarmed."

"I wish he had been armed," I answered, "for if he had been he would be alive today. I loved Sir Gareth, and I will regret his death all my life, for he was a noble, true, courteous and gentle knight. I did not kill Sir Gareth or Sir Gaheris on purpose or out of spite."

Then Gawain answered, "You speak fine words and make great offers which the King may accept if it pleases him. But I will never forgive my brothers' deaths, and if my uncle makes peace with you, I will leave his service, for you have been false to him and me."

"You have called me a traitor," I said, "and I cannot allow you to say that without defending myself."

"No, no," the King interjected, "you are under safe conduct and you may not fight. You will leave here as safely as you came. But, hear this. You may not remain in my kingdom more than fifteen days. If you remain in your castle, we will renew our attack, and this time, you will be destroyed along with all who support and defend you."

"Alas," I said, "that I ever came to this kingdom and that I have come to love and honor it above all others. It is a shame that I am banished without cause, but fate is changeable and the wheel of life turns. In spite of your banishment and what you say, I will return to my own castle and live on my own lands. And if you, my King, and my lord Gawain come to make war against me, I will endure it as best as I can. But, Sir Gawain, I warn you, if you come and accuse me of treason or crimes against the King, I will answer you with all my might."

"You may do your best," answered Gawain, "so run away as fast as you can, and we will come after you and bring your castle down around your head. Now, enough of this talk. Hand over the Queen and leave our sight quickly."

I turned to Guinevere and said loudly so that everyone could hear, "Madam, now I must leave you and this noble fellowship. But if you are ever oppressed by liars, send word to me quickly, and if any knight can rescue you, it shall be me."

Then I kissed the Queen and said, "Now let me see who dares to say that the Queen is not true to the King. Let me see who dares to speak."

No one said a word and I mounted my horse. Then, as tears flowed from Guinevere's eyes, I spurred my horse back the way we had come, with my knights following.

Guinevere was sent back to Londinium under guard. She had no choice but to await the outcome of the war between her husband and the man she loved, and to deal as best she could with the dangers that were on the wind.

As for Arthur, every day he rued, more and more, his obligation to Gawain, born of his own lies and guilt, and his fear for the safety of the crown on his head grew more desperate.

Chapter 19

Lionel had a squire named Bedoler whom he had recently knighted. Gawain's taunts were more than the young knight could bear and he defied my orders and left the castle to joust with Arthur's knights. Lionel feared for his safety and followed him. A skirmish ensued with three of the King's men. Lionel quickly and easily unhorsed one of them with his lance and turned to face and charge one of the other knights while Bedoler dealt with the third. As he turned, his destrier stumbled and, in the instant that he was unbalanced and defenseless, the knight who was charging at full tilt struck Lionel with his lance. Lionel wavered in his saddle for a moment and fell to the ground.

The sudden defeat of the famous and feared Sir Lionel brought the encounter to a sudden end. Bedoler leaped from his horse and ran to his mentor, screaming all the way for help. Squires and litter bearers rushed from the castle and carried him back to the chapel where surgeons were always prepared to treat the injured.

The knight who struck Lionel sat on his horse, unmoving as a statue. His helmet, in his hand, hung by his side and tears ran down his cheeks as he sobbed. Just months ago Sir Lionel had been a friend and a brother knight in the court of King Arthur. Now, because of the King's foolish jealousy, they had met as reluctant foes. The world had been turned upside down and, with Arthur and Lancelot at war with each other, the world would never be right again.

When I walked into the chapel, Lionel was already stripped of his armor and clothes and lying on a small, plain, bed. Blood pumped from a ragged and purplish wound in his left side. Three surgeons hovered and scurried around him attempting to staunch the flow with dressings and bindings, without any sign of success. Their worried expressions and air of defeat told me all I needed to know. Lionel's face was deathly white and he must have been in great pain but he remained calm and stoic while chaos surrounded him.

I pushed one of the useless surgeons aside and knelt by the bed. When I put my hand on his, Lionel turned his head to look at me and smiled. I had never seen anyone I loved so deeply in so much distress and a wave of fear swept over me. This was my cousin and the blood that drained from him was my blood. I wanted to take him in my arms and hold him so close to me that my strength and my life would flow into him and he would be healed. I would have done anything to save him, but I saw, with each passing moment that it was not to be.

Then Lionel looked beyond me and the look on his face became so calm and peaceful in a way that was not of this world. I turned and saw Bors standing at the foot of the bed. He held a small wooden cross in his clenched hands in front of his heart and his lips moved silently, in what I thought must be some prayer, as tears rolled down his cheeks. The thought came to me suddenly that, as close as we were, I did not know that Bors and Lionel were Christians.

The brothers stared deeply into each other's eyes for a short while and then it was over without a word spoken. I looked at Bors and saw only sadness on his face. I had expected him to be furious and filled with rage. But I was wrong. In that moment I understood that Bors had accepted his loss as the will of his god. If he would not turn to anger and hate and seek revenge then neither would I.

I left the chapel feeling as if I had lost a part of my life that could never be restored. Then I remembered something Merlin had told me many years ago.

"When someone you love has died, the tears you shed are not for the deceased, they are for yourself. They are tears of self pity."

I had loved Lionel and been blessed by his love and companionship all of my life. I would not debase his courage and greatness by crying for myself. I squared my shoulders and walked out from the dark chapel into the sunlight.

The siege went on this way for half a year. There were many injuries and deaths on both sides, as Arthur's men tried again and again to capture the city.

One day, Gawain came to the gate fully armed on a noble horse and carrying a great lance in his hand. He cried out in a loud voice, for all to hear, "Where are you now, you craven traitor, Sir Lancelot? Why are you hiding in holes and behind walls like a coward? Come out now, and I shall take revenge for the death of my three brothers."

Everyone in the castle heard Gawain's taunts and insults. My angry kin and knights drew around me and, as they hurled insults back at Gawain, Sir Palomides said, "Sir Lancelot, Sir Gawain has called you a traitor. Now you must defend yourself like an honorable knight or else you will be shamed forever. Now it is time for you to act. You have delayed too long and suffered too much."

Palomides was right. I could no longer ignore Gawain's insults and accusations. But even more, I was fed up with the situation. I had lost family and friends in this selfish and ugly conflict. Gawain had pushed me further than I was willing to go and the time for self-control and forgiveness was long past.

So, I ordered my strongest horse to be saddled and my arms to be brought to the gate of the castle tower. Then I called out to King Arthur and said aloud, so that all could hear, "My lord Arthur, I am sorry for your sake, that you make war upon me. I have tried to restrain myself for you. If I had been vengeful, I would have met you in the field and tamed your boldest knights. But, I have suppressed myself, and my knights, for half a year, and allowed you and Sir Gawain to do what you wished. Now I can endure it no longer and I must defend myself. Sir Gawain has accused me of treason. And though it is against my will to fight anyone of your kin, I can no longer refuse his challenge. I am driven to it like a hunted animal who is trapped."

"Sir Lancelot," Gawain answered, "if you dare to do battle, stop your babbling and come off that wall, so that we can ease our hearts' desire."

So, I went to the gate and was armed and mounted my horse and took a great lance in my hands. When I rode out of the gate, Arthur's army parted and moved away.

During the siege, many men-at-arms and knights who resented or opposed Arthur came to Joyous Garde. Where once we had only one hundred knights, we now had hundreds of soldiers and three hundred knights. All of them came out of the castle and town to see the battle between Gawain and me. When Arthur saw the great number of warriors opposed to him, he was amazed and realized that I had told the truth and that I had restrained myself for his sake,

Then Arthur announced that no man could come near Gawain or me or help either one until one or the other had yielded or was dead.

When we were ready, we rode apart to a good distance from each other, turned, and charged with all the strength and speed our horses could gather. We struck each other in the center of our shields with so much force that our horses reared up and were thrown to the ground.

We leaped free of our mounts and shouldered our shields. Then we stood face to face and Gawain struck so many fierce and bitter blows with his sword that, at first, I was very hard pressed to defend myself.

Neither one of us was as young and vigorous as we once were. Though Gawain was still as strong as a bull, he had grown heavy over the years, and he was no longer as quick and long-winded as he had been. I had lost some quickness as well, and many years of outdoor living and fighting had taken a toll on my bones and joints. But, I was as lean and strong as I ever was, and I could still fight furiously without becoming winded.

I allowed Gawain to beat on me for a while but after almost an hour I was unwounded and had nothing to complain about, except for a few minor bruises. I decided that the time had come to put an end to the exhibition.

"My lord, Sir Gawain," I said, "now I am satisfied that you have done all that you can against me. It is my turn to do my part and repay you for the insults you have heaped upon me day after day."

I attacked Gawain with all the speed and strength I could muster. As he backed away from me, trying to escape my assault, he lowered his guard and I struck him with such force that he crumpled to the ground and laid flat on his back, unable to rise. He covered his upper body with his shield but I could have killed him, then and there. Instead, I did not approach him or say anything to him. I just turned my back and began walking away.

"Why are you leaving?" cried Gawain. "Come back you false traitor knight and kill me. If you let me live, I will come back when I am healed and fight you again."

"I shall let you live," I said, "for the sake of my lord, the King."

I turned to Arthur and said, "Now have a good day my lord, for you will win no honor at these walls." Then I went into Joyous Garde, and Gawain was carried to King Arthur's pavilion, where leeches were brought to him, and his wound was cleaned and treated.

My sword stroke had gone through Gawain's left shoulder blade and into his left breast. Arthur was miserable because Gawain was so badly wounded, and he realized that the war was hopeless. He continued the siege with little enthusiasm for fighting, and I kept my men inside the city walls, so that they fought only when necessary.

As the siege continued, Gawain's wound festered, and he lay near death for a month. Then, desperate news came from Londinium that caused Arthur to end the siege. He put an end to it and ordered most of his army to march directly to Londinium while he commandeered boats, from the small fishing villages on the coast south of Joyous Garde, and set sail with one hundred knights and the injured Gawain.

When Arthur left Londinium with his army to attack me at Joyous Garde, he named his nephew, Mordaunt, as regent with the power and authority to rule the entire kingdom. Mordaunt had inherited his mother's hatred for Uther Pendragon and all his descendants, especially Arthur.

Arthur's war against me was unpopular with many nobles, knights and common people in the Kingdom. They loved and supported me and my kin for the many great and charitable deeds we had done, and for the peace we had brought to many places in the land. The war was also very costly to the people, whose taxes were raised, and there was anger at the King, for taking the flower of British knighthood to fight and die. So there were many people, both noble and common, who were opposed to King Arthur and were ready to follow another ruler.

The unhappy state of affairs in the kingdom, and Mordaunt's own quest for power, made him bold, and with the help of his own traitorous knights, he began a final plan to overthrow the King. To begin his revolt, Mordaunt had letters written and sent, as if from Joyous Garde, saying that Arthur had been killed in a battle with me. Now that he appeared to be the undisputed ruler, Mordaunt called the lords together and assembled a parliament, where he had them choose him as King. Then Mordaunt was crowned at Canterbury, where he held a feast for fifteen days.

Having accomplished the first part of his plan, Mordaunt then went to Londinium, took Guinevere into custody and brought her to Canterbury, where he announced that he would marry his uncle's wife. Guinevere was deeply distressed but she was determined not to marry Mordaunt and she made her own plans to defy him. So she kept her peace and did not oppose him in public or private. After the day of the wedding was decided, she asked Mordaunt to allow her to go to Londinium to buy the clothes and other things that were necessary for a wedding.

Because Guinevere had been so agreeable, Mordaunt trusted her and gave his permission. But, the Queen rushed instead to Tintagel Castle and prepared her followers to defend themselves. When Mordaunt learned how he had been tricked, he raged with anger. He sent forces to Cornwall to besiege the castle. But through many assaults, the castle stood firm and could not be breached. The Queen was safe from her husband's nephew, who she now recognized was her worst enemy.

Mordaunt had convinced many nobles and common people to believe that Arthur's leadership brought them higher taxes, war and strife, whereas he offered peace and prosperity. And so, the people, who were wanting in wisdom, never satisfied and easily swayed, decided that they were better off with Mordaunt as King than with Arthur.

When Mordaunt learned that the siege of Joyous Garde had been lifted, that Arthur had left most of his army to the north and was coming, with just a small number of knights, to Dover, he rushed to meet his uncle with a far superior force. He had gathered more than five hundred knights and an equal number of foot soldiers. When the two opposing forces met in a field between Dover and Folkestone, the battle was a horrible slaughter. Though he was barely alive, Gawain tried to rally Arthur's knights, but he was cut down and killed. As their numbers dwindled, Arthur's remaining knights gathered around his flag and tried to protect him. But, they were all killed, except for Sir Bedivere who was injured and laid hidden by corpses so that he was not found by Mordaunt's troops. Arthur was the last to die, slain by some unknown soldier.

Mordaunt's victory was not yet complete. He realized that as long as I was still alive, he would have no peace. Without waiting for the dead to be buried, he marched his army north to attack me at Joyous Garde.

There were fast riders who brought the news of the King's death and Mordaunt's plans to that remaining part of Arthur's army that was still on the march to the south. The Barons and noble knights gathered and agreed that they would not follow Mordaunt or allow him to usurp the crown of Greater Britain. As you know, they chose one of their own, your master, Constantine, who is now your Queen's husband, to be their King. Then they turned their march north, once more, to join forces with me at Joyous Garde.

When Mordaunt and his army arrived at the walls of Joyous Garde, they expected to continue Arthur's siege. But I opened the great gate, and more than one thousand knights and one thousand foot soldiers and archers poured out of the castle.

Mordaunt's army could not withstand the surge. As for me, all of my long lasting anger and passion was released in the slaughter and havoc that surrounded me. But, my killing was mindless, except for one burning desire, and that was to find Mordaunt.

The miscreant was hiding behind a phalanx of knights. I hurtled into them and they scattered. He remained where he was, sitting on his horse, holding the reins in both hands, motionless and looking forward. The thought came to me suddenly that, he was thinking that if he did not move, no one would see him. It was as if he was not really there. I could not see his eyes behind his helmet, but I stopped thinking and swung my sword, edge first, with every ounce of my strength. His body remained sitting firmly in his saddle as his head hit the ground and rolled away.

I had completed my own prophecy. I had killed all of Lot's sons.

Chapter 20

When Guinevere heard that Arthur, all of his knights, and Mordaunt and the rest were dead, she quietly left Tintagel and went, with five of her ladies, to the nunnery at Amesbury.

Fool that I was, I thought that every possible impediment to my love for Guinevere and her love for me was finally removed from our lives. I pictured our future being the one I had always dreamed of and hoped for, in spite of the impossible barriers before us. Arthur was dead. Mordaunt was dead. I had Joyous Garde, the most wonderful castle in all Britain. We would have friends and supporters to protect our safety and privacy. No King would ever be strong enough to threaten us. We could finally live as husband and wife with no dishonor or scandal.

I rushed to Tintagel but when I reached the castle, a warder, who was waiting for me, told me that she had already gone to take the veil.

I left Cornwall immediately, and rode hard toward the east for six days, until I finally reached the nunnery at Amesbury. As I walked through a garden toward the cloister, Guinevere saw me through a window, recognized me, and fell in a faint. When her ladies and gentlewomen revived her, she asked that they bring me to her.

When I entered the cloister, I saw her sitting with her head bowed low onto her chest. She slowly and unsteadily raised her head, and I could hardly believe that this woman was actually the Queen. She stood up with great difficulty, leaning on the arms of two of her ladies, and I saw how much she had changed. Her body, clothed in a dark habit, was slightly stooped. Her beautiful long hair, now streaked with white, was combed back under a white wimple. Her skin was pallid and her eyes were dull. No pleasure at seeing me was on her face. She looked at me steadily but the look was leaden.

Despite a quavering voice, she said just loud enough for all to hear, "This terrible war was caused by this man and me. We have caused the deaths of the flower of Kings and knights in the world. Through the love that we had for each other, my most noble lord and husband has been killed. Therefore, Sir Lancelot, I have come here to atone for my sins and cleanse my soul. I require you, and beg you with all my heart, for all the love that ever was between us, that you never come here again. I command you to forsake my company, and return to your Kingdom, for as much as I have loved you, my heart will not allow me to see you. Sir Lancelot, go to your own country and take a wife and live with her in joy and bliss. And pray for me so that I may amend my sins."

"Now, sweet madam," I said, "would you have me return to my country and wed a lady? No madam, that I shall never do. I shall never be so false to you. The same destiny that you have chosen, I will choose as well."

"I cannot believe," said the Queen, "that you will keep your word and not return to the world again."

"Well, madam," I answered, "say what you will, but you know that I have never broken a promise, and I will forsake the world, as you have done. You alone have been the cause of all my earthly joy, and therefore, Lady, since you have decided to live this life, I will find an abbot who will accept me and spend the rest of my life in penance. Therefore, madam, kiss me one last time before I go."

"No," said the Queen, "that I shall not do, nor can you kiss me."

I wanted to rush to her, take her frail body in my arms and kiss her with all the passion left in me. I wanted to tell her that we were not the cause of Arthur's downfall, merely the means. But, I knew that she would not respond to me and that I would only be forcing myself on her.

There was nothing left to do. I looked at her, trying to replace the vision before me with the young and beautiful Guinevere that I had loved. But, the effort was useless. The Guinevere of my golden years, of the time of my youth, was gone forever and I was no longer the young Lancelot. So, with great sadness, I turned on my heel and walked away.

There has been a holy place or monastery here on the coast, surrounded by the waters of the North Sea, for a very long time. The Celts built here first, long before anyone's living memory. They called their monastery Lindisfarne. I remember when the Christians came and destroyed everything that was sacred and replaced what they found here with their own monastery that they still call Holy Isle. I left the cloister at Amesbury and came here, six years ago, after forty-two winters and summers, because I was old and tired of being responsible for taking care of others and trying to meet all sorts of demands made of me.

I have been here ever since I last saw Guinevere.

I wanted to be left alone, in peace and quiet. This place was a good choice for me since it is only five miles from Joyous Garde. I do not want to be a burden or inconvenience to anyone and they will not have to carry my body very far, to my tomb, when I am dead.

We are isolated and peaceful here. The summers are mild but there are frequent winter storms that are very powerful. The waves crash and thunder against the sea wall and sometimes it sounds as if the gods are hurling boulders against the bulwarks. Whenever the wind is high it screams through the cracks in the walls, sounding like a banshee. But most nights, when the monastery is quiet, the only sound I hear is the sound of the surf pounding on the beach not so far away.

The only people here who new me in my old life are the abbot, who was once the Bishop of Canterbury and a penitent, who had once been Sir Bedivere.

When I first came here, I gave the Abbot a small fortune in gold and silver. In return, he agreed to let me live as I wished, without interference, as long as I did not cause any disturbance, have too many visitors or violate any rules of the monastery.

As you can see, Master Lonmarch, I do not live here in noble luxury. Like the monks, I work hard every day. I wash clothes and cook for everyone in the abbey. Depending on the season, I also do my share of plowing the fields, planting and sowing crops, threshing and baling hay. I have taken the vows of poverty, chastity and obedience and, by my own choice, I am subservient to the Abbot. The only dispensation I have is that, since I am still more pagan than Christian, I am not required to pray as the monks do.

I sleep on a straw-filled pallet in a cell that is just large enough to also hold a small writing table and chair and a small cabinet for a few spare items of clothing and small items that I still cherish and wish to keep until the end. One wall has a small unglazed window that looks out onto an herb garden that I plant and maintain. The stone walls are thick, and it does not get too hot in summer. But my cell is bitterly cold in winter with no fireplace for warmth and it is then that my body suffers most for my sins.

I have no real friends among the monks, not even Bedevere, and the only conversation I have with anyone else is about the work we have to do. During the day, I am too busy or tired to think, but when I am in bed, waiting for sleep, almost as in a dream, I see the past. I see the battles I fought, the men I killed, and the people I loved, hated and lost. I imagine that I see my father and mother. I see Guinevere and the other beautiful women I have known. I picture Galahad as a baby and as the knight I made of him seven years ago. I remember that I have not seen him since then and I do not know if he is still alive. I remember all of the mistakes and betrayals and terrible choices I made and then a dark, empty feeling comes over me and I see myself, a faded warrior, old and tired, waiting to die.

Merlin disappeared soon after Galahad was born. Everyone assumes that he died since, in everyone's memory, he was an old man. I choose to believe that he found some way to cheat Death and is still alive and performing his tricks somewhere. No one has heard a word about Galahad, Percival or Bors for years. Lionel, as I have told you, was killed at the siege of Joyous Garde. Fer de Blanc was put to stud many years ago. I have not heard from Niniane or Saraide since Galahad's birth.

Your King Constantine, is not well-loved and is ruling badly. I hear that the Saxons are once again on the move, and there have been several encounters where they have been successful against our armies.

There is nothing that I can do about this sad situation, and I hope to be dead and in my tomb at Joyous Garde before the Saxons reach this far north. After I am buried, they can burn Joyous Garde to the ground, and I will disappear beneath the stones and ashes for all time to come.

Poor Niniane's quest has gone for naught. I was a failure. It seems obvious that Galahad, if he is still alive, has not found the Grail, or Bran's head, since Britain is once again under attack by land and sea. So there is no magical salvation for the Britons. As for me, I still doubt that there ever was a Grail. The stories about invisible castles and drops of dried blood that can heal the sick and raise the dead are just that ... stories.

No matter how hard I work during the day, I have difficulty falling asleep at night. Lying on my cot, strange ideas come to my mind and blend with my memories. Sometimes I think that my life has been nothing but a long dream and I am just a storyteller who does not know how the story began or how it will end. I wonder; if life is really just a dream, will I be forgotten after I die, as if I never existed? Will dreamers of the future, remember me and tell my story to their children so that at least my story never dies? If my story is just a dream, then only if you are a dreamer can you pass it on.

Nothing about my life or my deeds has made a lasting difference in this world. Like me, everyone I fought, loved and hated, leaves this life with nothing more permanent than a ripple in a pond. Evil always outlasts good. War is the way of the world and peace is only a brief respite

Still, to struggle on in life is what we must do even if the struggle has no meaning. I was born to be what I was. I make no excuse or complaint. For a while, I was Sir Lancelot of the Lake, King Ban's son of Benoic. I was an honorable, courageous knight without equal. I did great deeds, helped the poor and never did harm to a lady.

What more can any man ask?

Chapter 21

On the sixth day I walked down to the beach at low tide and found the townsman waiting for me next to his skiff. He took my bags from me and stowed them as I climbed aboard. As he rowed slowly against the currents I looked back at Holy Isle and tears came to my eyes. I felt as if my heart would break and the better part of me would die if I left that place. I had pleaded with Lord Lancelot to let me stay with him but he would not let that be. How well he understood the love that men had for him who knew of his honor and courage, his prowess and gentility and all of the finest virtues of a gallant knight.

Alas, all that this poor man can now do, to repay the great trust he has shown in me, is to write his story truly and fairly. But with all of Queen Vyvyan's good will I know that the manuscript will never see the light of day. There are too many reputations to protect, too many lies to keep and too many old scores to settle to allow Sir Lancelot's story to be freely told.

I know what to do. I will give the Queen her manuscript but not before I make a copy. I will seal the copy up against wind, rain and fire and I will hide it as best I can, using all the cunning that my wit allows. Perhaps, some day, when all of us are long gone, some good-hearted soul will find my poor manuscript and having read it, will care enough, about a hero's good name, to show it to the world.